THE Roommate AGREEMENT

EMMA HART

NEW YORK TIMES BESTSELLING AUTHOR

Cover Design by Emma Hart
Editing by Ellie at Your Brother's Editor
Formatting by Alyssa Garcia at Uplifting Author Services

THE Roommate AGREEMENT

CHAPTER 1

You Must Wear Pants

Shelby

"**Y**ou! Shove this filthy, cheesy piece of crap up your ass!"

Jay turned his head, staring at me with wide green eyes, his hands firmly around the controller of his Playstation. "What?"

I threw the dirty sock at his head. "I've had enough! Three months, Jay! Three months! You told me you'd have another place by now, but I still just had to pick your dirty damn sock up out of the bath before I could shower!"

My best friend's eyes darted up and down my body. "Is that why you look like a clan full of cats just dragged you out of a forest?"

"It's a clowder."

"What?"

"A group of cats is a clowder." I paused, then shook

1

my head. "Not the point. I'm sick and tired of picking up after you. You're twenty-six! Why can't you work a washing machine?"

He paused his game then tilted his head to the side, flashing me his signature charming grin that did absolutely nothing but piss me off. "Because you know how to, Shelbs."

I grabbed his jacket from the back of the chair and threw it at his head. "I am not your mother! I am your best friend and apparently, your keeper, you overgrown man-child!"

"Whoa, whoa, whoa!" He grabbed the jacket before I hit him in the face with it. "No need to make more mess. It's bad enough as it is."

Annoyance flared within me. I stormed over to the living room and stood with my feet apart and braced my hands on my hips. Slowly and deliberately, I cast my gaze over the living room.

Over the empty bottle of Mountain Dew on the floor by his feet, the crushed Red Bull can on the side table with the lamp, the pizza box on the coffee table surrounded by empty food packets...

"And who does the mess belong to, Jay?" I asked in a deathly calm voice that my mother would have been proud of.

He froze, the grin falling from his face. "You sounded like your mom."

I continued to glare at him. "I am not picking up after you anymore. I'm tired of finding your clothes in the washer when I need to wash mine. I'm sick of picking up after your rubbish because your lazy ass can't find the trash can, and—hey! Are those my Oreos?"

"No!"

The tell-tale blue packet peeked out from between two packets of Doritos. I reached forward and snatched it before Jay had a chance.

It was my Oreos.

And the packet was empty.

"You ate my Oreos!" My voice was shriller than it should have been, but this day was going from bad to worse. I was behind on my deadline, there were dirty socks in my shower, and my shit roommate and future ex-best-friend had eaten my only pleasure in this life.

Jay had the good grace to grimace. "Sorry?"

"Sorry? Sorry? One thing in that kitchen is off limits to you, and that's my Oreos!" I waved the packet to punctuate my point. "They are the one pleasure I have in life!"

He winced. "They're just cookies, Shelb. I'll stop at the store and get you some more when I come home from work later."

I crunched the packet up in my fist and folded my arms. "And you're going to tidy your mess up before you go."

He checked his phone. "I don't really have time."

"You have time to play video games."

"Yeah, but I get to kill people in video games." He paused. "I can't kill anyone tidying up."

"You can kill the mess."

"Not the same."

"Okay, then I can kill you for coming into my apartment and wrecking it." I tossed the Oreo wrapper in the trash and went to the fridge for a bottle of water.

There weren't any.

Leaning back, I peered across the apartment at Jay. "Where's all the water?"

He hit a button on the controller and put it down in a scarce space on the coffee table. "The guys came over after you went out with Brie last night."

"Jay…" I groaned, slamming the fridge door shut.

He knew how I felt about that. In fact, I'd told him once a week, every Monday, ever since he'd moved in.

Jay worked for his dad. Wesley "Wes" Cooper owned a successful chain of gyms in Texas and had put his son in charge of one of them. Jay's friends consisted of sports-obsessed, beer-loving, wing-eating, gym-rat couch coaches.

And, lucky me, they converged on my apartment every weekend. Or they had ever since he'd moved in *temporarily.*

Since Sunday happened to be my designated day off to work on my own novel instead of ghostwriting or freelance news articles, it wasn't all that convenient.

Men watching sports were loud. Toddlers in a playground kind of loud. Not to mention that every single one of Jay's friends thought they were more qualified to manage the Dallas Cowboys than the actual coach.

Although they probably weren't far wrong at this point in the season. Especially in my dad's opinion—and that was something he gave whether or not you wanted it.

I digress.

I was more than a little fed up of having my quiet apartment ripped apart by men. All I wanted to do was write my book, wander around in yoga pants and tank tops with swearwords, and eat my body weight in chips and queso whenever the urge came over me.

It was hard to do that with judgey-ass gym-rats all over your living room.

Not that I cared. If there was anything better than chips and queso on the sofa, it was chips and queso in bed without pants on.

Now there was a quote for a t-shirt.

Still, I was tired of it. I wanted my apartment back. I wanted to not find socks in the bathtub and empty bottles under the sofa. I wasn't a freaking mom yet. I didn't need another person leaving shit everywhere, thank you very much.

Jay stood up and held up his hands. "All right, I'll pick it all up."

I folded my arms across my chest and eyed him. "Then you can vacuum the crumbs up from the carpet."

He paused.

He didn't know where I kept the vacuum cleaner. I bet he didn't even know where I kept the damn dishcloth.

I leveled my gaze on him. He knew that I knew he didn't know, but I also knew that he didn't want to admit it.

Jay was, if nothing else, a bit of an alpha male. If he were a character in a book, he'd be a werewolf alpha without a doubt.

He stood at over six-foot-tall, and his muscles were the perfect mix of toned and bulky at the same time. He wasn't going to be entering a bodybuilding competition any time soon, but he was the guy that made girls look once, twice, at least three times on the beach or, hell, on the street.

His hair was unfairly dark and thick, cut close to the sides of his head. The top was longer and swept over to the side. Coupled with a square jaw that was dotted with yesterday's stubble and startlingly green eyes, he was impossibly handsome.

But none of those looks would work on me.

I met him when he was missing his two front teeth and he'd punched a boy in fourth grade for being mean to me.

We'd been in first grade.

He'd taken a suspension, and I'd found myself a new best friend.

Nobody had ever bullied me since that day.

"You can look at me like that all you like, Jay Cooper. I'm not going to tell you where I keep the vacuum cleaner. Just like I'm not going to tell you where I keep the pods for the washer."

He groaned, grabbing an empty plastic bag from the cupboard to pick up his trash. "Come on, Shelbs, help me out here."

"No. If you want to keep living here, things have to change. You have to start picking up your fair share of the chores and you have to be more respectful of me." I gripped the edge of the island and leaned forward. "I'm tired of it. I'm tired of having my Sundays interrupted by your couch coaching. I'm sick of doing your laundry like I'm your mom and I'm sure as shit fed up of you eating all my damn Oreos."

"Always with the Oreos," he muttered, shaking the bag out with a noise that went right through me. "All right, all right. I get it. I'll pick up my shit now and make it up to you, okay?"

I grunted an unintelligible noise and pushed off from the counter. Storming into my bedroom—the only room in the apartment untouched by Jay—I slammed the door behind me for dramatic effect.

I did enjoy a good dose of drama—as long as I was the one dishing it out.

I had no time for it from someone else. Unless it was on Facebook and I could go down the rabbit hole of comments. Then I had time for it.

The fact was, my drama was warranted.

Three months ago, Jay had turned up on my doorstep the day before his apartment building was sold and begged to stay with me. His loose-tongued, Fireball-loving grandma had just moved into his old room at his parents' place, and he had nowhere to go.

I had a spare room and as a writer staring into the black hole that was my bank account, needed a roommate.

It had seemed perfect. He promised he'd be out by three months. That he was actively looking for a new place and he swore it wouldn't be too long.

I'd believed him. We'd been best friends for over a decade when we'd started high school, and he'd been the hot football star who needed tutoring.

And no, it didn't go the way most romance books did.

Instead of the book-loving girl making the hottest guy fall in love with her, we became best friends.

Now, that asshole was in my spare room, still not on the tenancy officially, and was eating all my goddamn Oreos.

Things had to change.

I had to face the facts: Jay wasn't going to move out anytime soon.

That wasn't necessarily a bad thing. I mean, I still needed help with the rent, so I'd just end up having to find a new roommate anyway. Keeping the pain in the ass one I already had seemed like less of a risk than trying to find someone else.

Besides, I had Jay's mom's phone number if he annoyed me too much, and I wasn't afraid to use it. Not to mention that the woman loved me; she often referred to me as the daughter she never had.

I wasn't sure if that was because she wanted me to actually be her daughter or if she liked having somebody else be 'bad cop' when she didn't like his girlfriends.

As the best friend, that was my job. Right? Weed out the weak and all that.

It had absolutely nothing to do with the fact I had a minor crush on him. Nope. Not at all.

Okay, maybe it did. But in my defense, the crush was relatively new. There's only so many times you can see your best friend wandering around in a towel, still wet from the shower before it starts to do things to you.

Namely, turn your clitoris into a little heathen.

Because let me tell you this: I do not need to get turned on while flipping pancakes in the morning. Or making a ham sandwich. Or cooking dinner. Or sweeping the floors because the man has the schedule of a two-year-old who's been left in charge of the day's activities.

Not like me. No. I like my schedule. I wake up at the same time, eat at the same time, work at the same time and, for the most part, sleep at the same time.

A bit like a cat.

No matter how anal Jay tells me I am, it doesn't change this: I work from home. If I don't have a schedule and set work hours, I'll spend all day lounging in front of the TV wearing last week's sweatpants and no bra while eating my weight in Cheetos.

Then I'd need three roomies to pay the rent, and I was just about coping with one.

I picked my phone up from where I'd left it on my bed and checked it. I had a ton of Instagram notifications, so I sat down and scrolled, clearing all of those before I checked my email.

I had an email from earlier this morning asking about my ghostwriting rates, so I tapped out a quick response with a note that I hoped to hear from them soon.

Two knocks rattled my door right as I clicked off the email app. "What?"

"Can I come in?" Jay's voice crept through the crack.

"Sure."

The door creaked open, and he poked his head through the gap. "I cleaned up. I couldn't find the vacuum, but I did find the broom and swept, so that's halfway there."

It wasn't, but I'd already gotten on his back enough today. "Thanks. I can vacuum soon. I have some work to do while you're out and it's quiet."

He nodded, pulling his lips up to one side. "I'll buy you two packets of Oreos on the way back from work. How's that for an apology?"

"It's a start," I replied, trying to glare at him, but my smile was too intense to fight. "Thank you."

"I'd say you're welcome, but I owe you." He shrugged. "I'm going to work. Do you need me to grab anything else while I'm at the store?"

"Do you know where the dishwasher tablets are?"

He stared at me like I was speaking Japanese.

I sighed. "Just water, then. Go to work, loser."

He grinned and did just that.

CHAPTER 2

Get The Fuck Off My Oreos

Shelby

B rie looked at me across the table, a fry dangling between her finger and thumb. "Really? Again?"

I nodded. "All my Oreos."

"Of course you'd focus on the Oreos and not the mess."

"Actually, focusing on my Oreos is the only thing making me not freak the fuck out about the mess." I paused, reaching for my cocktail. "I don't know if I can do it anymore, Brie. I don't want to kick him out, but I want my space back. I think he forgets who the apartment technically belongs to."

She dipped the fry into ketchup and shoved it into her mouth. "It's like having an overgrown child living with you, right?"

I nodded again, sucking on my straw.

"When Sean moved in, I wanted to claw out my eyeballs with a fork. He'd lived alone for so long that he had zero semblance of anyone else's space," she said, referring to her long-term boyfriend who'd moved into her apartment. "It's been six months, and honestly, he's only just getting it. I spent far too long hoping he'd just realize it before I broke down and set rules. I don't think he pays attention half the time."

"I shouldn't have to set rules. He's twenty-six. I've been complaining about it for almost the entire time he's lived there."

"Yes, but Jay's too used to living his bachelor lifestyle." She picked up her own drink and curved her black eyebrows upward. "And you're too used to living the introvert life."

"The introvert life is the only one worth living. No phone calls, no random drop-in visitors, I don't have to wear pants..." I trailed off because that wasn't entirely true.

Now, I had to wear pants.

It just wasn't the same when I was making pancakes. Pants were restrictive.

"Yes, yes, I know. I stopped dropping by unannounced when you answered the door in a thong and a thin tank top."

I shrugged. "I looked through the peephole. I knew it was you."

"It was fucking tactical, and you know it."

"Of course it was. I don't like surprise guests." I grinned. "Which is why it's so distressing when Robin Hood and his band of merry men descend on my living room to watch football. There isn't nearly enough space for all their muscles, never mind enough doors to block out their couch-coaching."

I was being a whiny bitch. I knew it. I also didn't give a shit.

"Tell me about it. Sean was there last night when we went to the wine bar. I found out when I got home to him being stupid drunk and yelling abuse at an invisible Jason Garrett."

I finished my drink. "Sounds about right. Jay admitted this morning that he'd had the guys around without telling me. I only knew because they'd drunk all my water."

Brie groaned, running her hand through her black hair. "They're such children. They have no respect."

"And that's the problem." I waved three fries at her. "He thinks he's being respectful, but he's not. I lost my shit at him this morning so I think he's starting to realize I can't keep living like this, but I don't know what to do."

Brie waved down our server and motioned for two more drinks. "You could call his mom. She'd have his grandma come around and beat his ass."

"Yeah, but then that puts me in Betsy's debt, and I don't think I have enough money to buy all the Fireball she'd demand."

We shared a smile. Jay's grandmother's obsession with Fireball wasn't exactly a secret in town, and it'd caused her to remove her shirt in public more than once.

I did not want to be the person who was responsible for that.

The entire town was still getting over the last time. Especially since Betsy, uh, favored letting the girls go free, if you know what I mean.

"Well, at the very least, you need to lay down the law," Brie replied, slicing her burger in two. "Lay out some rules or something that you both agree with. And, for the love of God, find out if he's going to stay permanently to get his ass on your lease."

With a sigh, I swirled a fry through the ketchup on the side of my plate. "I know. But I don't want him to think I'm forcing him to stay or kicking him out."

"Just tell him that you need a roommate. That's why you allowed him to stay anyway, wasn't it?"

"That and I'm not a heartless bitch who'd put him on the streets."

"Well, yeah, but it wasn't like he didn't have notice. He just thought everything would fall easily for him like it always has." She shrugged and sat back. "You need a roommate, and he clearly doesn't want to leave. But you have to make it official and set some rules."

I tapped my nails against the table. "All right. I'll give him two options. Sign onto my lease and live here properly with rules, or he has a month to move out. Or is that not enough time?"

"A month is fine. In the meantime, I'll find you a safe to store your Oreos in, just in case."

New drinks were placed in front of us, and we both grinned.

Now that was a best friend.

The apartment was deathly quiet when I got back. I checked the time and saw that Jay would still be at work for another hour, so I wouldn't see him until some time closer to ten.

If he remembered to stop by the store for my Oreos.

Not that it mattered. I'd wandered to the store on my way back walking home from the bar where Brie and I had met for dinner. I was now the proud owner of three different packets of Oreos, which meant I no longer got to wonder why my shirts were getting a little on the fitted side of life.

Look, writers didn't wear fitted shirts. We barely even wore pants unless they were sweats or yoga pants. We weren't here to look pretty; we were here to write until our fingers bled and we cried into our wine.

Nobody said it was a glamorous life.

Still, I'd gotten my work done before I'd gone for dinner with Brie and now I was happily under a blanket on the sofa in the living room. My shorts were made of soft fleece and were probably a little on the indecent side, but they had a super-stretchy waist, so they paired exceptionally well with my Oreos and my tank top that, for once, didn't have a cuss word on it.

And on the screen was a healthy dose of *The Big Bang Theory*. Namely, Sheldon Cooper and his spot.

I could relate.

I had a spot.

There was a puffy chair in the corner of my bedroom with a little footstool that was my most comfortable writing spot. It'd once been in the living room, but after I'd found men with sixty pounds of muscle on me using it as their seat, I moved it.

The cushion was molded to my ass, thank you very much. I didn't need someone with some tight-ass buns ruining the squishy mess mine made.

I tore open the second packet of Oreos—no, I had not eaten the entirety of the first one—and lay back on the sofa cushions. My introvert reveled in the silence of the apartment in these moments.

It was just me, my greedy ass with my cookies, and my favorite TV show.

This was the life.

You know, if I didn't have to pay rent.

Damn being an adult.

I settled in comfortably and watched as the episode rolled onto the next one. There's something so relaxing about watching a show you've seen a hundred times before. That was how I felt right now—relaxed.

I could easily fall asleep right here, but that would be pointless. Jay was the loudest human being known to man and he'd just wake me up when he came in.

I sighed. How was I supposed to sit and broach the subject of him still living here? Not only was he loud and messy, but he had the attention span of a hungry ant. Unless it was football, then he had an uncanny ability to sit still for the entirety of the game, blocking out everything but whatever the Dallas Cowboys were doing wrong in his humble opinion.

It was a weirdly impressive skill.

I pulled another Oreo from the packet and focused on the TV screen. Turning off my brain was hard, mostly because fictional people lived there and liked to tell me what to do, but I was also a chronic over-thinker.

Which was why I could barely focus on what I was

watching.

Groaning, I put the cookies on the coffee table and rolled onto my side. I reached for my water and, right as my fingers made contact with the bottle, knocked it off.

Damn it.

I picked it up from where it'd landed just underneath the sofa and returned to my lounging just in time to hear four words from the TV.

"Screw the roommate agreement."

It came followed by a sharp gasp—and not just the one from Sheldon.

There was one from me.

The roommate agreement.

That was it. That was what I needed with Jay. A roommate agreement that laid out the rules, that worked in both our favors, and that finally drew the line between what was acceptable and what wasn't.

Hot damn.

I ran to my room, grabbed a pen and a notebook, and got to work.

CHAPTER 3

The Washer Will Not Kill You

Shelby

I sat on the stool at the kitchen island and waited for Jay to wake up.

I'd gone to bed before he'd gotten home last night, and since he'd gotten in so late, I'd been able to run to the library to print out the agreement I'd spent half the night working on.

Yes, I had a printer and no, it did not like me. The feeling was completely mutual, it should be noted.

It was a piece of shit, and I'd told it so.

Now, I sat, chewing on a piece of toast, waiting for his ass to get out of bed and read this over. I didn't know how he'd take it, so I even had pancake batter waiting to make his favorite chocolate chip pancakes.

That's right. I was that friend. I'll kick you in the balls, but I'll cook for you to soften the blow.

It helped that I was a pretty good cook and that Jay could, well. He could just about do a Pop-Tart where breakfast foods were concerned.

I mean, there was nothing like saying, "Good morning! You need to go on the lease so you're actually liable for rent," like making pancakes and bacon.

I tapped my nails against the top of the island. The sound of a door opening was shortly followed by the sound of a second one closing. I knew it was two different doors because the bathroom door had a horrible squeak that rang out whenever it moved.

I waited. The sound of the flush came as I knew it would, and I also wasn't surprised when I saw Jay stroll into the kitchen in his underwear.

He yawned, reaching between his legs, and scratched at his groin.

I cleared my throat, clapping my hand to my eyes.

He froze. "Shit."

"Please put some pants on. I need to talk to you."

"Sorry. Hold on."

I kept my hand where it was over my eyes until I knew for a fact he was back and wearing pants. There was only so many times I could see him in his underwear, thanks to my stupid little crush on him.

So he wasn't wearing a t-shirt, but I needed him to wear pants. I could deal with some inner drooling over my best friend's abs if I really had to.

Also, the view was nice. I'd pay for it the way people paid to visit a strip club.

Pancakes and abs were the things dreams were made

of.

Unless the abs belonged to your best friend and room-mate. Then, they were off limits.

Sadly.

"What's up?"

"Are you wearing pants?" I asked, relieving the pressure over my eyes just a little.

"I'm wearing what you call pants, yes."

Against my better judgment, I looked.

He was wearing sweatpants.

"You're a dick," I said, pursing my lips. "Sweatpants are real pants. It's literally in the name."

"All right, but I'm still not convinced about leggings." He leaned over the bowl full of batter mix. "Are you making pancakes? What bad news do you have?"

"Okay, first," I replied, swiveling on the stool. "Leggings are pants, and if you can't agree with that, you're gonna need to move out."

"Fighting talk." He dipped his finger into the batter and licked it off.

I reached over and smacked him away from it. "Second, I don't have any bad news. Well, I hope it's not. I had an epiphany."

"Well, fuck. We're all in trouble." He grinned, his green eyes glinting with laughter. "What's up?"

I pushed the paper toward him. "I wrote a roommate agreement."

"A roommate agreement?" Jay quirked an eyebrow. "Do I need to start rationing you on *The Big Bang Theory*?"

I knew he'd bring that up.

"There is nothing wrong with my enjoyment of *The Big Bang Theory*."

"You say enjoyment; I say unhealthy obsession..." He trailed off and shrugged.

"Says the guy who watches sports all year round and acts like the players can hear him yelling," I replied shortly. "No, this agreement is for real. It's not some joke, Jay. You've been here three months, so unless you're actively going to move out, we need to make sure the living situation is acceptable for us both."

He dipped his finger back into the batter and jumped back before I could hit him again. "You mean I'm going on the rental agreement."

"That's one thing, yes, but otherwise..." I shrugged. "It's how we're going to co-exist. We're different people. I like it to be quiet and calm and not have a club of bulking gym-rats yelling at the TV."

His lips twitched.

"You like life a little louder and more action-packed. I like everything to be clean and tidy, and you have no problem living in something a little messier. If you're going to move in permanently, we need something in place that keeps us both in line."

He walked around the island, taking the agreement with him, and leaned over. "All right, I'll bite, Shelbs. What kind of things am I going to find in here?"

I sat up straight. "Compromise. I won't complain about your friends invading the living room every Sunday as long as it is only confined to one day a week, with prior notice, and you make sure to replace whatever food or drink they clear out."

"You'll complain."

"I won't. I'll leave the apartment and work in Java Hut, or I'll go to Brie's or my mom's or something." I met his eyes. "I swear. That's part of the compromise, Jay."

He scanned the front page. "What else?"

"Little things. Like you picking up your socks."

"Fine, but you're going to have to make sure the drain in the shower is free of your hair."

I held up my hands. "Deal. There's actually a section in that for you to write down what you want me to do, and we'll compromise from there."

He made a low humming noise, one that sent a little shiver down my spine. "You're not allocating bathroom times like that lunatic on the show does, are you?"

"Sheldon Cooper is not a lunatic. He's a genius." I paused. "And no. I reserve the right to take a shit anytime I want."

He dragged his finger down the front page. "Ah, yeah, here it is. 'Jay will use the air freshener to make sure the bathroom doesn't smell like man after every visit.'"

It was my turn to grin because he'd made that whole line up. "You do stink."

"You don't exactly smell like roses after your morning trip to the bathroom. Neither does the damn room itself."

"Whatever. Anyway, the first thing in the agreement is the most important and actually related to this morning."

He flipped open the first page and looked at it. "You wrote it out like rules?"

"Damn right I did."

"Rule one: must wear pants," he read. Slowly, he looked up at me with raised eyebrows. "Was it necessary to put that in capital letters?"

"Were you or were you not in your underwear when you walked into the kitchen five minutes ago?"

He clicked his tongue. "Point taken." He continued to scan the page. "Really? You wrote about the Oreos as rule two?"

Getting up, I walked to the bowl of pancake batter that was on the counter and turned on the stove so the skillet heated up. "Yes, I wrote about the Oreos. They're important to me. But look—rule four is all for you."

"We'll ignore the part where the washer apparently won't kill me—you haven't proven that either... Sundays are for football? That's a rule I can get on board with."

"You should. It's not in there for my benefit." I sniffed and ladled some mix into the skillet.

"Are those for me?"

I slid my gaze his way. "Depends. Are you going to use a duster?"

"This says it's my friend, but I don't think it is. I think that's you trying to make me clean." He raised his eyebrows and put the agreement on the island. "I have to work this morning so I can't read it now, but I've got time to eat a pancake or eight."

I rolled my eyes. For a guy who probably had zero body fat, he could eat like nobody's business. He'd fit right in with The Rock on cheat day, except Jay would eat like that every day if he could.

"You'll take four, and you'll cut open the packet of bacon while you're at it."

"You want me to make the bacon?"

"Do I like my bacon crispy? Yes. Do I want it to be so burned not even Hell will take it? No. Get the frying pan and sit down."

"Yes, Mom."

There was a knock and the sound of everything in the pan cupboard collapsing seconds later.

"Shit."

"I am not turning around. I am not turning around," I muttered, flipping the pancake to do the other side.

I really wasn't going to turn around and look. I already knew that the precariously-organized cupboard was a collapsing hazard, and that was the reason I never, ever asked Jay to get anything from it.

Apparently, I'd been wise.

Until today.

But really, the damn frying pan was at the front. How he created a landslide of bowls and cookware… That was a special talent.

I didn't need to look to know how much of a mess it was.

Or that I'd be the one cleaning it up.

"I got it," Jay said, leaning over and reaching to put the frying pan on the hob right as I lifted the first pancake from the skillet and grabbed the ladle to make the second.

"No, it's fine. Just stack it on the counter, and I'll re-organize it. I've to do it anyway." I shrugged a shoulder and focused on the pancakes.

"You know you don't have to do everything, right? I can put the pans back." His tone held more than a hint of amusement. "You're cooking. I'm capable of being an adult, despite what you may think."

"It's not what I may think, it's what I've seen," I replied. "Hence the reason we have a roommate agreement."

"Can you stop making good points? It's really hard to agree with you if you're always fucking right."

Laughing, I removed the second pancake from the skillet. "Buckle in, Jay. You're always going to be wrong in this apartment."

"I'm re-thinking living with you." He stood up, lips tugged to one side. "I'm used to being right, and I'm not sure I can deal with always being wrong."

"It's going to be like that forever. It's in your DNA to be wrong. I'm sorry I have to be the one to tell you that."

"No, you're not. You don't look sorry at all."

I grinned, meeting his green eyes. "I'm not. Hey—look at that. You were right!"

His eyes shone with laughter, but he schooled his expression into one of annoyance. "If you weren't cooking me breakfast right now, I'd storm into my room."

"Ah, food. The great equalizer." I bit back a laugh. "Can you start frying the bacon while I finish these pancakes? Just flip the rashers when I say, and you won't cremate them like last time."

Jay sighed, sliding between me and the island to the other side where the frying pan was. He splashed some oil into it, which immediately fizzed in the heat of the pan. "I did not cremate them. They were nice and crispy like they should be."

"There's a difference between crispy and burned." My voice was dry as I added another pancake to the stack. "You burned them. I make them crispy."

He snorted but didn't say anything else. I kept casting glances over at the pan to make sure he didn't burn my bacon—he could have his burned if he wanted, but he wasn't going to sacrifice my bacon like that.

"Take mine out!" I flipped the final pancake onto the stack. "Now, Jay!"

"Wow," he said, taking the pan off the heat. "Is this the kind of nagging I can expect now that I'm officially going to be a tenant here?"

I glared at him and split the pancakes in two, giving myself the extra one. "It's the kind of nagging you've been getting since you moved your lazy ass in here; it's just that you're actually listening to me this morning."

"Ah, so that horrible noise that sounds like cats fighting in an alleyway has been you nagging me this entire time?"

I set our pancakes on the small dining table and sent yet another dark look his way. "You know, I can poison pancakes when I make them."

"Yeah, but then you'd have to pay all the rent again, and that's the only reason you're letting me stay here despite your better judgment." He grinned and joined me with the bacon, then slid my plate across the table toward me with a wink.

Keeping my glare in place was impossible when he was in this mood. Playful and borderline flirty was Jay's sweet spot, and it was how he got out of trouble with just about every woman in his life.

Except his mom.

I smacked my lips together and kicked at him under the table. "Brat."

"Yeah, but you love me." His grin widened as he grabbed the syrup bottle from the center of the table.

And that was the problem. I damn well did love him, and unless I got a handle on my little crush, I'd probably be *in* love with him, and that wouldn't be a good thing.

Nuh-uh.

No way.

And it was time to stop thinking about my totally inappropriate crush on my best friend.

I cleared my throat and took the syrup to put on my pancakes. "So. This agreement. You don't think I'm crazy?"

"Oh, you're crazy," Jay said around a mouthful of food. "But I already knew that, and I still moved in."

"You moved in because you waited so long to find a new apartment you were about to be homeless."

"Good point. But still, I could have moved in with Sean."

"And Brie would have killed you."

"Another good point." He clicked his tongue. "I know you're crazy, Shelbs. Sane people don't have voices in their heads or mutter to themselves as they wander around the apartment."

"What else am I supposed to do? Let the fictional people take over? Do you know what would happen if they were allowed to assume control of my brain?" I tapped my temple. "Anarchy, Jay. Anarchy."

He pointed a rasher of his over-done bacon at me. "If you're trying to convince me you aren't crazy, you're not doing a very good job."

I snatched the bacon from his hand and threw it at him. He laughed, throwing his head back.

He was such a shit.

"Are you done?" I asked after a minute, stabbing my fork into my pancakes.

He wiped under his eyes.

Was he crying? Oh, my God, he was. He laughed so hard he cried.

It wasn't even funny.

"I hate you." I put my bacon on the plate with my pancakes, grabbed the plate and my cutlery, and stormed off to my room.

He was insufferable.

CHAPTER 4

Sundays Are For Football

Jay

I knew she was trying to make a point.

The worst part? She had one.

I was a terrible roommate. Living on my own made me lazy, and it was easy to forget that Shelby was my polar opposite. I could handle mess, but it made her antsy.

Unless it was the desk in her room. That damn thing was the messiest fucking thing I'd ever seen in my life, but God forbid anyone tried to organize it.

She swears blind it's organized chaos.

I just think it's chaos, personally.

Everywhere else had to be tidy. And clean. God, it had to be clean. She could smell a watermark on a glass from the laundry room downstairs. I swear she'd once gone into the bathroom immediately after me to bleach the toilet and spray the room.

Still, she was my best friend. She had been for as long as I could remember, and I understood that it was her apartment and she liked things her way. We clearly couldn't live together without making a shit ton of compromises.

Which was why I was sitting on the sofa with ESPN on in the background, looking at the fucking roommate agreement.

I meant it when I asked her if I needed to ration her on *The Big Bang Theory*. It was clearly where she'd gotten the idea from, and it was absolutely ridiculous that she'd actually made one in real life.

Even if it was a good idea. Something I'd never admit to her. The last thing I wanted her to do was to start thinking that she was normal.

Last month, on a deadline, she chopped a pencil into a salad and stuck a carrot behind her ear.

She hadn't noticed that I'd thrown it out and made a run to the grocery store.

That's when I knew she really was crazy.

Still, I was going to humor her. I'd read her little agreement, sign it, and really try to be a better person to live with. I was also going to offer up some of my own suggestions because no matter how fair Shelby thought she was being, this was going to be skewed in her favor.

If I had to pick up my socks, she had to stop leaving her bras all over the place.

I didn't need any more encouragement to think about what she looked like not wearing them.

Wanting to see her naked was an unfortunate side effect of being her roommate, that was for sure.

Never in my life had I been attracted to her until I moved in. Not that I was blind to her—she was beautiful, in my opinion, but I'd never really wanted to grab her face and kiss her when she pouted in annoyance.

That...

That was a recent development. One that I wasn't entirely sure I was comfortable with.

So yes. She needed to pick up her damn bras.

I sighed and leaned back on the sofa, opening the agreement up. She'd stapled the damn thing together and everything. I was half tempted to pick up my phone and text her to see if she had a lawyer look it over, but she was at her favorite café writing.

And you did not want to interrupt Shelby when she was writing. Not if you wanted to keep your balls, and I most definitely did.

Instead, I smirked as I scanned the first rule. *Must wear pants.* She'd written it in big, bold capital letters and underlined the word 'must' three times. Thankfully, this was a rule I whole-heartedly agreed with. As comfortable as I was while just wearing boxers, this applied to us both.

Shelby had a habit of running to the bathroom in her underwear when she thought I was in my room. I'd caught a flash of her white ass more than once as she sped down the hall, and all that did was put my dick in an uncomfortable situation.

Lusting after your best friend was more hassle than it was worth.

I clicked the pen I was holding and skipped to question two. This one was also in capital letters: *Get The Fuck Off My Oreos.* I just about choked on my own spit as I continued reading.

Jay will ensure that he does not eat Shelby's Oreos. If he does, he must replace them within twenty-four hours with the added interest of one packet of double-stuffed Oreos.

Laughter burst out of me. What was she going to do, put a label on each packet to make them hers?

Actually, you know what? That wasn't a bad idea. I drew a little arrow pointing to this section and wrote that down at the side of the page. How else would I know which ones were hers? And the answer of "They all belong to Shelby" was, sadly for her, not the right one.

By now, she should be keeping them in her room. It's not my fault if she leaves them in the cupboard and I'm hungry.

Like I said: put a label on them.

Compromise, see?

Rule three: The Washer Will Not Kill You.

That was debatable. I didn't know how to use the damn machine, so there was, in fact, every chance it might kill me. It wasn't that I was a lazy-ass guy who'd never done any of his own chores, but my old apartment building was just that—old. It didn't have a laundry room, and my grandma wouldn't hear of me using a launderette, so she'd washed my clothes once a week when she'd dragged me around for dinner.

All right, it hadn't been dragging since she was an amazing cook, but still.

I sighed. This rule was one I couldn't actually argue with. She had been taking my laundry down with hers and leaving it on my bed when it was dry, and that wasn't fair.

In my defense, she just kind of took it out of the basket and did it.

Again, see the fact that she didn't like mess. Apparently, clothes in a laundry basket was mess.

I guess it was time I learned how to use the washers and dryers in the laundry room in the building. And where the room was.

I didn't say I was perfect.

Rule four was a rule I could get firmly on board with: *Sundays Are For Football.* They'd long been a point of contention between us, mostly because a bunch of guys in her living room didn't exactly help her when she had to work.

Not to mention that Shelby hated football. In fact, she despised it. She gritted her teeth every time she left her room to get water or whatever.

She'd already given me a general idea of this rule this morning, so I settled in and read what she'd written, cringing a little at some of it.

*Sundays are for football. During the on-season, Shelby will leave the apartment to work if the **Dallas Cowboys** are playing and the game is on television.*

That was specific.

The only exception to this rule is for the Super Bowl, regardless of the teams in it.

Right. Because the Cowboys were going to win the Super Bowl, weren't they? *Fucking hell, woman, don't get my hopes up like that.*

I carried on reading.

Arrangements can be made for other sports on Sun-

days during the off-season. If a sports event falls on any other day of the week, Jay will leave the apartment and find an alternative place to view it.

I winced.

Yep.

There it was.

The zinger.

Jesus fuck, she was striking a hard bargain with this.

Breach of this agreement will result in a one-month ban of football from the television.

My lips twitched. It was as if she was writing a fucking child's rule list out. A monthly ban? What was I, five?

I scratched that last one right out. The rest of it wasn't exactly bad. It was frustrating on a personal level, and that made me sigh and run my hands through my hair, but it wasn't unreasonable. Keeping it only to Sunday was fair since she was the one who had to move her office for it.

I scribbled a note to negotiate the games—one a week regardless of the team wasn't unfair—and moved on.

Rule five: The Feather Duster Is Your Friend.

I stopped.

What in the ever-loving fuck was a feather duster? Was it some kind of bird-based cleaner? Would I be cleaning the floors with a headless ostrich or something?

The lock on the door clicked, and it swung open, revealing a wind-swept Shelby hugging her laptop bag to her stomach.

I ran my gaze over her. Her dark hair was a disaster with strands of it flying in every direction, including over her face. Her cheeks were flushed and pink, and she blew out a long breath between her lips.

"Did you get into a fight with a tornado?"

She jerked her gaze toward me, blinking at me for a second. "No. I went to Java Jam on the front. It wasn't bad when I got there, but the winds really picked up about half an hour ago."

"Is there a hurricane coming?"

Slipping the strap of her laptop bag over her head, she said, "A hurricane? In May?" She rolled her eyes. "Just a regular storm coming in, probably. That's what the forecast says anyway. What are you doing?"

I sat up straight and put the agreement down as she smoothed her hair back from her face. "Reading the agreement through. I just got to rule five."

"The feather duster?" Her brown eyes scanned my face.

I did my best to keep my expression blank. "Yep."

She paused. "You don't know what a feather duster is, do you?"

"Well. I can't say I've ever used one, but I'm imagining cutting off an ostrich's head and using its body to clean the floors."

Shelby stared at me, her expression flat. "I have no idea how you've made it this far into adulthood without seriously hurting yourself or someone else."

"What? Because I don't know what a feather duster is?"

She turned on her heel and walked to the small closet in the hallway that I'd never opened. She pulled on the door, reached inside it, and pulled out a long stick. One end of it was covered with a rainbow of… I didn't actually know how to describe it. It was bushy and looked soft; at least in the areas that weren't looking a little on the gray side.

"This," she said simply, "is a feather duster."

I looked at it then her. "But it doesn't have any feathers on it."

"You took that literally?"

"I just told you I thought you wanted me to use a headless ostrich to sweep the floors, and you didn't think I took the word 'feather' literally?"

She raised her eyebrows. "Actually, I was hoping you just weren't that stupid."

I showed her my middle finger. "I've seen that before."

"Why didn't you use it, then?"

Shrugging, I got up and walked to the kitchen for a bottle of water. I shut the fridge and turned back to her. "Not gonna lie, Shelbs, I thought it was some kinky as fuck sex toy."

"How on Earth do you confuse a feather duster and a sex toy?"

"The stick. The fluffy stuff." I shrugged once again. "It's not like I know what you're into in the bedroom, is it?"

"Who the hell uses a feather duster as a sex toy?"

"Hey, some people might be into that. I mean, I'm not one of them, but for all I knew, you were."

My best friend looked at me with confusion shining in her eyes. "You are so freaking weird."

"From the person who talks to people who don't exist? That's a bit rich."

"Hey." She whirled on me, brandishing the feather duster as a weapon with it pointed right at my chest. "I know I'm weird. It's the people like you who don't admit it who are the ones we need to watch out for."

I rolled my eyes and sat back on the sofa. Sure. I was the weird one; not the girl who wandered around in tiny shorts, without a bra, her hair a mess atop of her head at six a.m. on a Sunday.

Aha. That was another one.

Decent clothes.

I scribbled that on the agreement.

Shelby shut the door with a click and peered over at me. "What are you writing? If it's permission to use the feather duster as a sex toy, the answer is no. Unless you buy your own, but if you haven't figured out where the laundry room is yet, I doubt you'll find where to buy one."

She was as funny as a car crash, this one.

"Hilarious," I drawled. "No, I'm making amendments as I go. I added a new rule."

"You added a new rule?" She raised one dark eyebrow and walked over, hovering over me. "All right, what is it?"

"Decent clothes must be worn. Do you know how many times I wake up early on a morning to open the gym and find you basically in your underwear in the kitchen?"

"Basically in my underwear? Who are you seeing in the kitchen? I wear shorts and a tank top at the very least."

"Yes, but the shorts barely cover your ass, and you're sure as hell not wearing a bra."

She paused, eyes glittering as she said, "And why are you looking at my ass and my boobs?"

That was an excellent question.

"Because there's nowhere else to look!" I rushed out before my stupid cock could get any ideas. "Look, waking up in the morning can be challenging for a guy."

She stared at me.

"I don't need to get up for a coffee with… you know." I motioned to my groin. "And see you half-clothed."

She flicked her hair over her shoulder and walked to the kitchen, turning her back to me. "Why does it matter? I'm your best friend. I hardly think your little friend is remotely interested in whether or not I'm wearing a bra."

Yeah, well, he is.

"Fine. If I have to wake up and see your perky nipples prancing around the kitchen, I'm going to stroll around in my underwear so you can get a good view of my morning glory."

She spun, lifting up a finger. Her cheeks were flushed, and she had to swallow before she could speak. "My nipples do not prance. They are not horses."

I grinned.

"Also, I have no desire to have anything to do with your morning erection, much less get a good view of it, thank you very much."

"Have I told you that you're cute when you blush?"

"Have I told you that you'd be a cute dead guy?"

I laughed, leaning back on the sofa. "C'mon, Shelbs. We need to respect each other's privacy. You don't want to see my cock hard over your breakfast, and I don't want to see your nipples standing to attention when I make a coffee."

She sighed. "Why did I ever let you move in again?"

"Because I was going to be homeless and you're the best friend ever?"

"Mm." She grabbed her coffee from the machine and leaned against the counter, cradling it against her chest. "Okay—fine. I accept that. What other changes have you made?"

"Every Sunday is a sports day, no matter the team or sport."

She clenched her jaw. "I suppose that's fair."

"That killed you to say, didn't it?"

"Get on with it before I kill *you*."

I chuckled. "You either have to put a label on your Oreos or keep them in your room, or I'm not responsible for eating them. If I don't know they're yours…"

"You're just being a picky little bastard now."

"Hey, I'm only on rule five. You're the one who made… what? Twenty-five-ish of them?" I shrugged and picked up the pen, giving it a pointed click. "Now it's my turn."

She sighed, dropping her head back. "I knew I'd regret this."

CHAPTER 5

The Feather Duster Is Your Friend

Shelby

I typed the treasured two words that made me feel like magic at the end of every manuscript with a sigh.

They'd feel more magic if this book belonged to me, but alas, this was paying some of the bills this month.

I saved the document and opened up my email account, ready to compose a new message to send the book to my ghostwriting client. It wasn't my favorite way to earn money since I was trying to get a stronghold in the industry myself, but my own books and the random bits of freelance work I got from local newspapers didn't earn enough to keep me in Oreos, never mind my apartment.

This particular client was an easy one for me—she sent me the bones of a draft, and I picked it apart and put it back together again. I didn't know much about her except that she loved to write but her day job got in the way, so she sent every book to me to fix up.

THE *Roommate* AGREEMENT

I liked it. I didn't have to use much brain power and I got a nice chunk of money in my bank account every two months.

I sent her the book with my usual message that I loved the story and was looking forward to the next one, sent it, and scanned the rest of my emails. After responding to one asking about my pricing, I clicked the one from a local paper I'd written for before.

They wanted me to do research into a supposed haunted hotel in the middle of the next town over and write up its history. They'd pay me, plus my gas to drive there, and it sounded like fun. I confirmed with them I could do it and cleared the junk emails out.

The front door opened. I glanced at the clock; Jay had the early shift today opening the gym, and holy shit—was it past lunch already?

Ugh. Apparently, Jay wasn't the only one who needed an adult.

The door shut a second later. I paused, raising my eyebrows, then shrugged and grabbed my basket full of dirty laundry.

Yes, I needed to eat, but I also needed clean panties.

I paused only to grab the detergent and fabric softener from the cupboard under the sink and made sure I had my keys to get back in. The elevator was on the floor above, so it was quick to get me and take me down to the ground floor, where I stepped out with the basket on my hip, turned a corner, and took to the small flight of stairs that led to the basement.

The shiny, tiled floor of the small hallway leading to the laundry room was slippery thanks to my slippers, and I

41

almost ended up on my ass before I hit the door.

Then, I froze in the doorway.

Jay was standing on the other side of the room in front of an empty washing machine. His hair was sticking up as if he'd just run his fingers through it and—yep, there it was, he was running his fingers through his hair. His tank top hugged his muscular torso, showing off his strong shoulders and unfairly lickable biceps.

Roving my eyes farther down his body, I lingered over the gray sweat shorts that hung low on his hips, just giving a tiny peek at the waistband of his Calvins.

"How can this be so fucking hard?" he muttered, scratching the back of his neck. "I can drive a car with a stick, but not operate a fucking washer."

Eyeing the basket full of clothes on the machine next to him, I let my lips curl into a smirk. "Well, it helps if you put the clothes *in* the machine."

He jerked, turning to look at me. "Fucking hell, Shelby, you scared the shit out of me."

I grinned and joined him at the back of the small room. "What's up? Can't find the power button?"

Jay rolled his shoulders. "It's complicated."

"Yeah? Is getting detergent also complicated?" I shook the box from my basket.

"Didn't think of that," he muttered, this time cricking his neck.

Aw. He was embarrassed.

"Careful," I said, leaning over and hitting the power button for him. "You're gonna blush in a minute."

"God, I hate you."

THE Roommate AGREEMENT

"All right. You figure it out by yourself." With a shrug, I took the only other empty machine in the room, two down from him, and went through the motions on autopilot.

He watched me tossing everything in and pushing all the buttons until I was finally done, put down the lid, and set it to start.

Then, I smiled at him, propped my basket back on my hip, and made my way out of the room.

"Shelby!" His pained voice carried into the hall.

"Yes?" I said sweetly, taking a few steps back to look at him through the door.

He turned his bright green eyes my way. "Will you please help me figure out the machine?"

My tongue darted out over my lower lip. "That killed you, didn't it?"

He ground his teeth together, but that was his only answer.

I laughed and walked back in, setting my basket down by the door, but grabbing the detergent and softener. "Look. It's simple. You have to turn it on here," I pointed to the light, "to open the lid."

He opened the lid.

"Now put your clo—whoa, whoa, hold up. You can't put those socks in with the red shirt."

He held a pristine pair of white socks in his right hand and the red shirt in the left. "Why not?"

"They'll go pink."

He eyed them. "Are you sure?"

"I'm sorry. Are you teaching me how to use the washer, or…?"

With a sigh, Jay put the socks back into the basket. "Okay. Fair point. Don't put whites with colors."

"Or darks. You should do three loads a week."

"Three loads?"

"Or you can toss them in together and get pink socks. Your choice."

"Three loads it is." There was a slight grumble in his tone, and by God, he would be a terrible househusband.

"Now measure the detergent and softener and put them in, too." I handed him the box and the bottle. "Use the cap on the bottle for that, and you'll find a little scoop in the box before you ask."

I took a step back and watched as he side-eyed me before he did it. He added the detergent and softener with more hesitance than a grown man should before putting them off to the side.

"Now set the temperature setting three and make sure the other dial is pointing toward cotton, shut the lid, and press the little button under the power one."

I fought laughter as I watched him. Honestly, I wished I had my phone to record this and send it to his mom to use in a video compilation somewhere. It was great entertainment.

Jay finally put down the lid and pressed the button. He actually jerked as the machine clicked to life, and I dipped my chin, almost suffocating myself as I held in my laughter.

"Congratulations," I said, my voice wavering with amusement. "You've made it twenty-six years and finally done your own laundry!"

He turned around, glaring at me. "I'm annoyed it was that simple."

This time, I didn't fight my laugh as I grabbed the laundry things and put them back in my basket. "What? Did you think you needed to offer the blood of your firstborn, sacrifice a goat, and dance naked on the roof to get it to work?"

"No, but if that will shut you up, I might just do it."

I reached back and punched him in the arm. "Nobody wants to see you naked on the roof. Or anywhere else for that matter," I added as the elevator doors dinged open.

"You say that, but it wasn't my personality that made the new girl give me her number today." He grinned, reaching over me to hit the button for our floor.

I rolled my eyes, ignoring the annoying little pang of jealousy that hit me. It had no business here, thank you very much. "You can't date employees. Remember the last time Keegan hit on a new employee? He didn't think through the hitting-and-quitting thing."

"Yeah, but Keegan isn't a gentleman like me."

I snorted and stepped out of the elevator. "You? A gentleman? When was the last time you did anything remotely gentleman-like for anyone?"

He held up one finger, darted in front of me, and put his key in the door before opening it for me. Then, he held it, sweeping his arm out for me to go in first.

I shot him a withering look and walked into the apartment, shaking my head.

"Just then," Jay added, following me inside.

"Doesn't count," I sang, putting the basket down and going into the kitchen. "You did that to make a backward point. You're not a gentleman."

"How do you know that?" He leaned on the island, resting on his forearms. "Are you the gentleman police?"

"No. I'm a woman with eyes," I said dryly. "Also, the basic understanding of what a gentleman is."

"Yeah, well, you're no lady. I've seen you eat pizza and scratch your ass at the same time."

"Aha." I pointed my teaspoon in his direction. "I, however, never claimed to be a lady. If I was, I would have washed my hair at some point in the past five days, and my sweatshirt wouldn't be two days old."

Jay paused, then slowly grimaced and nodded his head. "Right. I have to do my own laundry, and you can't even wash yourself."

"I wash myself. I shower every morning. I just don't wash my hair. Buns were created for lazy bitches."

"I'll never understand women."

"And that's why you're single and live with your best friend."

"Shelby, *you* are the reason I don't understand women."

"More fool you if you're using me as the benchmark." I shrugged and pulled last night's leftover pizza from the fridge, grabbed a slice, and tore a big bite off to prove my point.

Jay glanced at the box. "Your diet sucks."

"You ate more pizza than I did last night," I reminded him, turning the box around. It held four pepperoni slices and two of his vegetable pizza. "Who the fuck puts vegetables on pizza? If I wanted to eat healthily, I wouldn't be eating pizza."

"I hate it when you use logic on me." He leaned over and grabbed one of his cold slices. "Makes it hard to live with you."

"You chose to move in." I shoved the last bite of pizza in my mouth.

He paused to look at me for a second before shaking his head.

Again: I never claimed to be a lady.

I grinned, grabbing for my coffee. "How was work? Apart from being hit on. I know that was probably the best part of your day."

"Nah. She's not my type."

"Why? She blonde?"

"And taller than me. It's a double-whammy."

I choked on my drink. "You're the size of a tree! How can she be taller than you?"

Jay shrugged, snagging the second piece of his pizza. "I don't know, but she is. She's gotta be like six-four or something."

"You're six-foot-three. Is an inch really that much of a problem?"

Slowly, he pulled his lips to the side. "You're the woman. You tell me."

I choked on the bite of pizza I'd just taken, spitting it out into my hand. My throat was sore, and I knew my cheeks were the brightest red they'd probably ever been.

"No," I finally eked out, throwing what was in my hand into the trash. "The only people who have problems with inches are men and hair stylists."

"Whatever you say, Shelbs. For the record, no, I don't have an issue with one inch, but by the time she wears heels? Ouch." He shook his head. "Nah. It's far better to date short girls like you."

"Is it now?"

"Yeah. It doesn't matter how high your heels are; you'll still be small enough to throw over my shoulder." He winked at me, pushing off the counter.

"You lift a short girl over your shoulder and see what happens!" I called after him. "Our legs are just short enough to kick you in the dick!"

He stopped and backed up a little, smirking at me. "If a girl is over my shoulder, she's not gonna be kicking my dick. She's gonna be—"

"La la la!" I yelled, dropping my pizza to cover my ears. "La la la la la!"

He grinned at me until I let my hands fall away and quickly said, "Fucking it."

I clenched my jaw. "Not in this apartment!"

CHAPTER 6

Lock. The. Bathroom. Door.

Shelby

"So he signed it?"

I nodded at Brie, pulling my cocktail toward me. It was the weekly official girls' night, and two hours ago, Jay had officially signed The Roommate Agreement.

"And he didn't freak out?" Her dark eyebrows raised into perfectly-plucked arches. "Didn't go crazy?"

"Nope. We negotiated some points"—like me having to put my name on the Oreo packets—"and he signed it plus the tenancy agreement earlier. He always paid the rent to me anyway, but still."

"You like everything in its place." She grinned, her bright red lipstick making her blue eyes seem brighter. "What about dating? Is that in there?"

I sipped my drink. "Yep. Neither of us will bring one-night stands or casual sex partners back to the apartment. If either of us dates someone long enough to have them stay over, we'll handle that then."

"Is that because you'd want to cut a bitch or because you respect each other?"

"I would not want to cut anyone who slept with him," I said tersely. "I simply have no desire to hear it happening in the next room."

"Yeah, and you don't think about having a dance with his disco stick, do you?"

"Don't ever refer to a penis as a disco stick again."

"Oh, so Lady Gaga can do it, but I can't?"

That sounded about right. "Yes. And I don't want to do anything with his penis."

Brie snorted, taking a long sip from her glass. "Right. I'm sure you don't. How is that little crush of yours, by the way? Still going strong, or has it crawled back under the rock it came from yet?"

Two best friends were too much. I was going to have to cut them loose.

"Okay, we're not talking about this." I sighed and finished my drink, motioning to the server for another round. "The rules in the agreement are there for a reason. No more shirtless wandering around, he has to wear pants, and if he wants to stroll around the apartment in a towel after a shower, he has to make sure I'm either working or not at home."

"Really? All those rules and he *still* doesn't know you make googly eyes at him?"

"I do not make googly eyes."

"The lady doth protest too much."

"The lady doth talk too much," I shot back.

She met my gaze and held it for a second, then filled the air around our table with her loud laughter. "The lady doth talk too much, but it only bothers you when I'm telling the truth."

"It doesn't bother me. It's not the truth. I'm fine. It's fine. I don't have a crush."

"Have a crush on who?" A shadow fell over our table, and my heart skipped a beat as I turned my face.

Blue eyes. Dark-blonde hair. Muscular build.

"Sean. Jesus." Brie put her hand on her chest. "Are you trying to kill me?"

"Sorry, babe." He leaned forward and kissed her before taking the empty chair at our table. "Who has a crush on who?"

"I have a crush on Nick Jonas," I said quickly. "Uh, what are you doing here?"

He motioned to our drinks. "We're getting a drink."

"We?" Brie leaned to the side and raised one eyebrow. "Don't you know this is girls' night? What the hell are you doing here with one of your minions?"

"Minions? I take offense at that."

I groaned at the new voice, slowly turning my head to the side. "What," I said, "Are you doing here?"

Jay grinned, motioning for me to move over so he could take my seat. "'Sup, bestie?"

I stared at him. "No."

"Aw, come on, Shelbs. We wanted a beer and some food."

"No."

He sighed and walked around to the empty chair on the other side of me. His knee nudged mine beneath the table at the same time his elbow did above it. "I thought we'd come to celebrate the fact I officially live with you."

"Really? I was here commiserating about it," I muttered, making Brie snort her drink up her nose.

Our drinks were brought over, and the guys ordered theirs while the server was here.

"One night a week," Brie said. "That's all we want. Three measly hours."

"Two weeks ago, you both rolled in the door at two a.m."

I held up a finger. "Not our fault. We got wrangled into a bachelor party, and they wouldn't let us go. We explained this."

"If your parents didn't own this place, I'd be terrified of that," Sean drawled, looking at me.

All right, yes. We came to the bar my parents owned. We did that because, uh, hello? Free cocktails in exchange for covering a few shifts?

No. Freaking. Brainer.

"Excuse me?" Brie leaned back and gave him a look that said he better have a damn good reason for saying that.

She was sass personified. I didn't know how Sean coped with it, to be honest.

Mind you, I wasn't exactly Miss Polite.

"Drunk people can be crazy," Sean started. "And men at a bachelor party? They can get a little out of control because they expect strippers."

He was reaching now.

"Are you calling me a stripper?" Brie's tone was quickly getting dark. "It's that, or you don't trust me."

"I'm not—fucking hell, how did this happen?"

I leaned into Jay. "This is why you don't come to girls' night. We're here to complain *about* you, not to you."

He turned his head so his lips were close to my ear—a little too close. "I said it was a bad idea. He wouldn't listen. I think they had a fight."

My eyebrows shot up as Sean leaned into her and said something into her ear.

Brie looked at me, her nostrils flaring. "I need some air. Can you order my usual for me?"

"You want me to come with you?"

"No." She shot a look at Sean and slid off her chair, heading for the door. Her flat ankle boots squeaked against the floor, and Sean buried his face in his hands.

I looked at him. "What did you do?"

"Why do you assume it was him?" Jay asked.

Their beers were brought over, and we all ordered our food, including me ordering for Brie.

"Because he's a man and I'm a woman, so I'll naturally assume he fucked up," I explained. "Now, Sean, spill it."

He blew out a long breath and met my eyes. "We had a fight. Stupid shit. We're still adjusting to living together. Little things all piled up, and I thought being here would be helpful."

I pushed my empty drink to the side and finally pulled my full one toward me. "Bad idea," I said simply. "She

53

needs time. Trust me. I know how hard it is to move in with someone."

"Don't look at me like that!" Jay slammed his bottle onto the table. "I'm not that fucking bad!"

"You eat my Oreos *and* you are the reason we have a roommate agreement!" I slapped his forearm. "You are a terrible roommate."

Jay looked at Sean with a flat expression. "You see the shit I put up with? Does your roommate hit you? Does she abuse you for accidentally eating her Oreos? Does she make you sign a contract to keep living there?"

"That's called a rental agreement," I snapped.

Sean looked between us. "Are you both sure you're not married?"

"Over my dead body," I said right as Jay choked on his beer.

"Whatever. What do I do to fix this with Brie?"

"Well, to start," I said. "I'd apologize for implying she's either a stripper or that you can't trust her. That's the easiest way to find your ass sleeping in your car to-night. Then, I'd start with saying that you'll leave as soon as you're done eating. Tomorrow, I'd make her breakfast with her favorites then buy her flowers."

Jay leaned forward and looked at Sean. "That shit is why I'm single."

"Yeah, that's the reason." I rolled my eyes. "Seriously, Sean, whatever you did, just talk to her. Now, before her food comes out and she's really hangry."

His lips twitched. "You're right. I'll go and apologize and promise to leave after we've eaten. Thanks, Shelbs."

He got up and walked to the door right as my dad came over.

"What's up, kids? Did girls' night change?" He wiped the table and looked at us both with kind blue eyes.

I shook my head. "Our security was breached. Who let them in?"

Dad laughed when Jay scowled at me. "We'll do better. What's up with Tweedledum and Tweedledee out there?"

"Living together issues," Jay answered. "I can relate."

Once again, I rolled my eyes. "Did you replace my Oreos?"

"I'll do it tomorrow!"

Dad's chuckle was deep as he grabbed our two empty glasses. "Jay, son, all these years and you're still eating her cookies? Didn't you learn not to do that in fourth grade?"

"You'd think," I muttered.

Jay knocked his elbow against me. "Shut up, you. This is why we have a rule that you have to label the packets."

"You're still gonna eat them!"

Dad looked between us with an expression of disbelief on his face. "I have no idea how you two have lasted this long as friends, much less live together."

I raised my glass. "I'll drink to that, Dad."

"Same." Jay clinked the neck of his bottle against my glass. "If anything is worth drinking to, it's that."

Hear, hear.

I groaned as I stumbled into the kitchen, holding my head. "Drugs," I muttered, gripping onto the island. "I need drugs."

I was speaking into an empty room because I knew for a fact Jay was still in bed. He hadn't managed to shut his door before he'd passed out on his bed, fully-clothed, at one-thirty this morning.

That, and I could hear him snoring from here.

He was like a fucking horn bringing boats into a harbor.

With my eyes half-closed, I felt my way through the room to the drawer with the drugs with my head pounding. If I felt this bad, I hated to think about how bad Brie felt. I'd been drinking water along with my mom's lethal cocktails, but she hadn't been.

She and Sean had made up sometime during dinner, and since everyone apparently had a day off tomorrow, the drinks had flowed.

I'd pretended not to notice when Sean and Jay had slipped some money into my mom's back pocket. So had she, even though she'd giggled at their not-so-stealthy attempt.

There was a chance Sean might have stumbled and grabbed her ass while he was slipping a couple of twenties in there...

I found the ibuprofen and shook the bottle. Good. It wasn't empty. The cap was tough to unscrew, but I managed to get it off and shake out two pills.

Once I'd taken them, I left another two on the counter next to the cooker for Jay and got him a glass of water. There was no way in hell he'd have enough mental capacity this morning to get his own. Kind of like a baby bird.

Opening the fridge door, I stared inside. I wasn't sure what I was actually doing looking inside it, but I needed to eat before I headed to the library to do some research for the haunted hotel article. If I didn't, I'd fall down the rabbit hole of research and never come back out.

Well, I would. Just not in any decent amount of time.

I hummed and pulled out some yogurt and berries. That would do for now. If I had anything heavier, I'd probably throw it back up.

I stifled a yawn and tipped some of the yogurt and mixed berries into a bowl to eat. I was halfway through it when Jay wandered into the kitchen, looking a hell of a lot more awake than I thought he would be.

Without speaking, I pointed behind me to where I'd left him a helpful little present.

He walked past me without acknowledgment, and the next noise was the sound of the glass being put back down on the counter. "Thanks. I needed that."

His voice was raw and husky, full of sleep, and far sexier than it had any right to be.

"You're welcome," I said around a mouthful of fruit. "How do you feel?"

"Like I need some of your food."

I wrapped an arm around my bowl and pulled it into me, glaring up at him. Damn it, even with his hair sticking up in all directions and the imprint of his sheets on his cheek he was still hot.

He was also shirtless, and while it was against the agreement, I just… didn't have the heart to tell him to put a t-shirt on.

What?

I was only human.

He had abs for days—the perfect, lean kind that screamed kale was one of your food groups but also said that you liked pizza and beer. His entire body was perfectly molded, from his strong shoulders to his tight chest and that tantalizing 'v' that curved over his hips and sent girls wild.

"There's plenty more left," I said, using my other hand to push the pot of yogurt and berries toward him. "You're not eating mine."

"Are the berries frozen?"

I shook my head. "I took them out of the freezer yesterday and forgot to put them back, but they're super cold."

He grunted, grabbed a bowl, and joined me at the small island. "How do you feel?"

"Better than I thought I would. I was drinking water, too, though. You?"

"Dehydrated," he replied, shoveling a spoonful of food into his mouth. "Not as bad as I thought I would feel, either. I woke up and drank like three bottles of water after you went to bed."

"See? I'm a good influence on you. Three months ago, you'd be the walking dead the morning after drinking."

He pointed the spoon at me and nodded while he chewed.

I smirked and got up, grabbing two bottles out of the fridge. I slid one his way and uncapped mine.

Then watched as Jay drank the entire bottle in one go.

"Are you a walking desert or something?"

He laughed, choking on the final mouthful, and knocked his fist against his chest. "Told you—dehydrated. I might have to go for a run in a bit to sweat this hangover off. Wanna come with?"

"Run? With you? Are you trying to recreate The Hare and The Tortoise so that the tortoise loses dismally?"

He laughed again, knocking his elbow gently into mine. "No. I promise you—twenty minutes and you'll sweat most of it out. Otherwise, you're gonna feel dead by midday."

"I don't know. Running in this heat with a hangover sounds like the quickest way to kill me."

"I'll keep it in mind."

Rolling my eyes, I scraped the last of the food from my bowl and put it in the sink. "Good to know."

"Seriously, Shelbs, come running with me. We'll go down to the front, run along the pier, then come back."

I side-eyed him. "You promise?"

He mimed crossing his heart. "I swear on your Oreos."

"Don't swear on my Oreos. They're not yours to swear on." I paused. "If it's longer than twenty minutes, you owe me two packets."

Jay finished his breakfast, even going so far as to lick the spoon clean. "You know that's counter-productive to a run, right?"

I shrugged, grabbing my water. "I'm not running to lose weight. I'm running to sweat out a hangover. Oreos are a perfectly good post-run snack."

"Yeah, well, don't complain at me when you can't fit

into your pants!" he called after me.

"I won't have to! My pants have a stretchy waist!"

"Leggings aren't pants!"

"Wash your filthy mouth out with soap!" I shouted back, slamming my door for effect.

Still, I heard his laugh.

His stupid belly laugh that rumbled across my skin in goosebumps.

Ugh.

Crushes were for schoolgirls and movie stars.

Not your best friend.

CHAPTER 7

Always Apologize With Pizza

Shelby

Running while hungover was not for the faint-hearted.

I was safely ensconced in the library with a hundred years' worth of papers and magazine articles, a packet of double-stubbed Oreos, and a bottle of water, and I was still hating myself for agreeing.

Jay could run. Fast.

Me?

Not so much.

I couldn't have been much slower. Despite the constant side-eye he gave me for my fitness, which resulted in me thinking about which pair of shoes I should wear when I ram my foot up his ass, I just didn't want to be there.

It was warm but raining. Not even real rain. That stupid light drizzle that feels foggy and not all that wet, but ultimately turns you into a drowned rat after five minutes.

It was horrible.

I wouldn't admit that it'd gotten rid of my hangover, but it had. Mostly, anyway. The horrible tight feeling in my forehead had gone, and I did feel better for pushing my body a little. I was still dehydrated, but since it was past lunch and Brie still hadn't replied to my texts, I was pretty sure I was in the better shape of the two of us.

The papers that were in front of me were all copies. There were several reports of what the media called genuine hauntings, but there were also several theories that it was all a marketing ploy.

I had the horrible feeling I'd have to spend a night there myself in their most "haunted" room to get any objective answers.

I didn't have the money for this, and I doubted the paper would dig into their pockets for a hotel stay.

Maybe I could convince Brie to come with me. Hmm.

Then again, she was a big baby who'd once been spooked by her own shadow, so that probably wasn't going to happen anytime soon.

I'd have to think about it. Maybe calling the hotel themselves would get me some results.

For now, I filed the copies into a clear file and tucked it into my backpack to take home. There were a ton of things to go through, and it'd take far more than one day.

I zipped up my backpack and made my way out of the library, waving at the elderly librarian, Viola, who'd been here as long as I could remember.

It was only a couple of blocks to my apartment, and the rain had stopped, so I set out into the dreary, dull Texas afternoon and turned the corner to step onto the road that would take me back to my apartment.

I stopped at my favorite café on the way to get some pastries and ready-made sandwiches because there was no way Jay had cooked—he'd either gone back to bed or was playing video games and scratching his balls.

Why did I have a crush on him again?

It was a great mystery.

After adding some pie to my order, I paid and took my bag full of goodies the two blocks to the apartment.

As I'd suspected, Jay was sitting on the sofa, bent forward, jamming his thumbs onto the controller in front of him. He didn't look at me as I came in, but he did jerk his head in my direction in acknowledgment.

I set the bag on the island and unloaded it, waiting until he'd groaned in frustration to speak. "Did you eat? I got lunch."

The sound of buttons tapping filled the air, then he got up. "What did you get?"

"I got you a tuna sandwich." I handed him his and grabbed my BLT.

"Yeah? What's the rest of it?" His green eyes sparkled as he looked at the other boxes in the bag.

I murmured something under my breath, but I wasn't going to give him the satisfaction of knowing that my diet really was worse than my fitness.

He laughed, pulling out the clear cartons and locating the apple pie. "If my sweet tooth wasn't as bad as yours…"

I jerked my leg out, going to kick him, but he'd already moved toward the cutlery drawer and grabbed himself a fork.

"Day off. Hungover. I can do what I want."

I eyed the sofa as I opened my sandwich. "At least you're wearing pants this time. The last time I came home to you on that stupid thing, you were scratching your balls like a two-year-old just discovering his penis."

"Discovering your penis is a highlight of a man's life. Discovering how useful it is, is even better."

"That's far more information than I ever needed to know." I took my sandwich over to the sofa and sat next to him. "And I don't want to know anymore."

Laughing, he saved his game and shut the PlayStation down, making it so the TV came back on. We scrolled until we found a show we both agreed on—in other words, a rerun of The Big Bang Theory that I wanted to watch—and set the remote back on the coffee table.

"Are you telling me," Jay said around a mouthful of food, "that little girls don't discover their vaginas when they're toddlers?"

"Not really," I said vaguely, picking a bit of tomato out of my sandwich. "The first time I really cared about it was… well, aside from puberty and the perils of becoming a woman, it was when I discovered my clit."

He choked on his sandwich. "Really?"

"Yeah, and if the past is any indication, I'm still the only one who's ever found it."

That didn't help his choking. It made it worse, actually. He banged his fist against his chest until I leaned over and smacked his back a few times.

"Too much information," he croaked out, putting the sandwich down and reaching for some water. "Way too much, Shelby."

"Now you know how it feels," I said smugly, settling into the corner of the sofa. "I don't want to know about your penis any more than you want to know about my clitoris."

Except I kinda did, didn't I?

Ugh. This roommate thing was not working out. Why had I asked him to sign the tenancy agreement again? This was only making my crush worse, and that really was a problem since I'd seen him at his worst.

Cheeto-dust on his chest, scratching his balls, needing a shower like yesterday kind of worst.

Which meant that my crush was an even bigger problem.

Nobody was attractive while covered in Cheeto-dust.

Take it from me. I'd had enough late-night writing sessions to know that for a fact.

Yet, here I was, still crushing on him.

I needed to move out.

"What are you muttering about?" Jay side-eyed me.

"Nothing," I said quickly. "There's too much tomato in this sandwich, that's all."

"You're so picky. Make your own sandwich in the future."

"I buy you lunch on my meager artist wage, and this is how you repay me?" I sniffed. "That's the last time I bring you pie when you still need to replace my Oreos."

"Oh, my God, I told you I forgot!" He turned his bright green eyes on me. "Fine. I'll go to the store this afternoon and get your damn Oreos, okay?"

"Roommate agreement says you owe interest." I smirked.

He clicked his tongue and sighed. "I'm going to regret signing this, aren't I?"

"Hopefully."

Brie: I think I'm dying.

I raised my eyebrows at the text that popped up on my phone screen. Picking up the phone, I unlocked it and hit the bubble to reply.

Me: Did you just wake up? It's four in the afternoon!

Brie: No. I woke up, threw up the contents of my stomach, went back to sleep, threw up again, and just woke up from a second nap.

Me: You should have listened to me about drinking water.

Brie: Sorry, Mom. Maybe you should take my drink from me next time.

Me: I tried. You almost threw it over me, so I gave up.

Brie: Ugh. I'm sorry. It was a rough night. Hell, it's been a rough day.

Me: What happened?

Brie: We fought last night, and he left for the gym without talking to me.

I frowned. They'd been okay all night at the bar after she'd stormed out—what the hell else happened?

Me: I'd call you, but I don't want to hear you throw up. What happened?

Brie: I might throw up if I have to talk.

Brie: It was stupid. They had this new girl start at the gym, and I knew they'd all exchanged numbers, but she kept texting him all night.

Uh-oh.

Brie: Every time you guys were talking or left us alone, he was on his phone, replying to her. Like he didn't want to be alone with me or something.

Me: Oh, Brie.

Brie: We got home, and he was texting even when I was trying to unlock the door. Keyholes move when you're drunk, btw. I confronted him, and we had a huge fight. He slept on the sofa, and that's it right now. He hasn't come home yet, he ignored my calls, and won't answer my texts.

I frowned. He wasn't even supposed to be in the gym today. I knew that because there was no way either Sean or Jay would drink that late if they had to work the next day.

You couldn't give someone a personal training session if you were hungover, could you?

Me: Let me ask Jay. He can probably get ahold of him.

I slid my chair out from under my desk, took off my headphones, and pulled open my door. "Jay?"

No answer.

That was a no, then.

Still, I poked my head into the living room and kitchen and gave a cursory glance toward his room. Nothing.

I pulled up the text thread again and detoured to the bathroom. May as well pee while I was up and all that. I told Brie that Jay wasn't here, but I'd call him and see if he could find him.

It probably wasn't the most soothing thing I'd ever said to her, but there was a reason I was never an agony aunt for my high school newspaper—or the college one, for that matter.

I wasn't always the most sympathetic person in the room.

I pushed the bathroom door open and stilled as I slammed into a wall of moist air.

And there, standing in the middle of the bathroom, butt naked, was my best friend.

Jay froze, clutching the towel in his right hand, and my

eyes did a quick flick up and down his body of their own accord.

I did the only thing I could do.

I screamed.

Slammed the door behind me.

And ran into my room and slammed that door, too, only just catching Jay's shout of, "Shit!" from the bathroom.

My heart thundered against my ribs. I'd just seen Jay naked—completely naked. No pants or underpants or towels hiding his modesty. No, the towel had been firmly in his hand as he'd dried off his thigh, but that didn't mean I'd missed everything else.

I hadn't missed the way his dark hair had flopped over his forehead, dripping down onto his face and body. I hadn't missed the way water droplets had cascaded down his body, using the dips and curves of his toned stomach as their own personal playground.

And I sure as shit hadn't missed the way they'd run right down over the 'V' muscles that pointed to one very specific body part.

His cock.

His semi-hard cock.

And it hadn't been because of the water temperature, because last I knew, hot water didn't make cocks hard.

Then again, I wasn't a man, so maybe they did, but still.

Part of me wanted to storm out of my room and demand he cleaned the shower, but the other half of me wanted to stay in here and only come out to forage for food when I knew he wasn't home.

There was no way I could look him in the eye again.

Why was he semi-hard? Was he getting himself off in the shower? Why hadn't he locked the door?

If he was getting himself off, who was he thinking about?

Oh, my God. Did it matter?

No.

It wasn't my business. I didn't care who he thought about when he fondled himself. He was a grown man who could think and tug any time he liked.

He didn't need my permission.

Why was I even thinking that?

Why did I have to open the door?

Damn it, Brie, if I hadn't gone looking for him, then I wouldn't have found him. And found a hell of a lot more than I needed to.

I didn't want to know what Jay looked like naked.

All right, that was a lie. I did want to know, but I didn't want to, you know, *know*.

Imagining it was so much easier. If I could imagine him naked, I could give him a flaw. Like... wonky testicles or a really, really tiny penis. Maybe an unfortunately placed mole or scar or something.

Now, though?

No.

Now, I was shit outta luck. He didn't have wonky testicles—not that I could see, anything. There were no sadly-placed moles or scars or spots.

And his penis was most definitely not really, really

tiny. Not even really tiny. Not even just tiny. Or mediocre.

Nope.

If it were a machete, you'd be able to take down forests with it.

Thank God penises were, as a rule, ugly. Otherwise I'd really be able to romanticize this moment.

There was nothing romantic about it.

There was nothing more awkward than walking in on your best friend totally naked.

Your best friend who you had a crush on.

Whose disco stick you kinda totally *did* want to take a ride on.

Two knocks at my door made my heart skip a beat. "Shelby? Are you in there?"

If I stay quiet, will he know?

"I was being polite. I know you're in there."

Guess so.

"Can I come in? We need to talk."

We really, really don't.

"Shelbs."

I sighed. He wasn't going to leave me alone. "It's not locked."

Gently, he tested the handle, almost as if he thought I was lying to him. The hinges creaked as he pushed it open and poked his head through the crack. "Hey."

I ran my tongue over my dry lower lip. "Hey."

"Can I come in?"

I nodded, tucking my feet beneath my butt and leaning against the headboard. "Sorry. About that." I jerked my shoulder in the direction of the bathroom.

"No, listen." He ran his hand through his still-wet hair, pushing it back from his handsome face. "It's my fault. I knew you were in here working so I didn't even think about locking it since I knew it'd be quick. Sorry."

"It's both of us. I had my headphones on and must have taken them off when you were already out of the shower. I blame Brie."

He drew his brows together, perching on the edge of my bed.

Not a place I needed him to be when my heart was still calming down.

"Brie? What does she have to do with this?"

I quickly explained the situation that she'd told me about. "I called for you, but I guess you didn't hear."

"No, I didn't. Shit. He wasn't scheduled to work today." He chewed on his lower lip, and I wanted to reach out and pull his lip from between his teeth because, well, lips that pretty weren't meant to be nibbled on.

Except by someone else.

Preferably me.

Whoa—what was this? One glance at his penis and suddenly I'm choreographing getting him under my sheets?

Geez.

I needed a vacation.

"You want me to try to call him?" Jay leaned back and rested on his hands, turning to face me. "He might know why I'm calling, though."

"Could he be at the gym still? Uh—is the new girl working today?"

He shook his head. "She's training under me. She'll be in tomorrow when I get there."

Ugh.

Damn it.

Not my business.

"Where could he be?" I asked, pushing a wisp of hair behind my ear. "Brie was drunk, and that doesn't excuse what she accused him of, but it was pretty shitty behavior. I don't know, Jay."

"You think we should keep out of it?"

I hesitated. "They're our best friends, but…"

He raised his eyebrows, lips tugging up at one side. "They're adults and have to sort out their own relationship issues?"

"Something like that." I deflated with a sigh. "Maybe try calling him. If he picks up, tell him Brie's worried about him and wants to know he's all right."

"What if he doesn't want to go home?"

"Then you can make up the sofa for him and bring me pizza to apologize for the unexpected house guest."

He stared at me for a moment then burst into laughter. "You'll use any excuse for pizza."

"Wine would be good, too. And—"

"Oreos. I know." His tiny smile became a full-fledged one that made his eyes light up.

My tummy flipped.

"Don't worry. I'm on it." He reached out and flicked

my ear. "By the way, I think your scream deafened me."

I wrinkled up my face as he headed for the door. "Yeah, well, seeing you naked scarred me, so we're even."

His laughter followed him out of the room.

I wished he'd taken my attraction to him with him.

CHAPTER 8

Bras Do Not Live On The Sofa, Shelby

Jay

"**Y**ou think you can handle it?" I turned my head to meet my new employee's eyes.

Georgia nodded, her blond ponytail swaying as she held her finger out and pointed at everything on the counter. "Let the phone ring two times before answering, people coming for the first time need a forty-five-minute guided tour of the machines before they can go alone, the schedule for classes is in the calendar, and the price list is right here." She finished by tapping the price list. "I got it. You can go for lunch. One hour alone isn't going to kill me."

"All right. Are you sure?"

"I have your number if there's a problem."

"I won't be far. Just down the street. I can be back in two minutes."

"Stop panicking!" She laughed. "It's not like I'm here

alone. Lisa's over there and, uh…" She paused, her finger hovering in the direction of the tall, heavy-built black guy who was currently instructing a young woman on how to use the treadmills.

"Liam," I said, lips twitching. "Lisa and Liam. Are you sure you can remember?"

"Yes. I'll be fine." She smiled at me.

"All right. See you soon." I knocked on the counter and left the main floor of the gym, heading for the staff room and the lockers there to get my phone and wallet. Sean was already waiting for me in there, and he looked rough as hell.

"Took you long enough," he grumbled, rubbing his hand through his hair.

"That's a lot of thanks for someone who gave up his sofa and had to spent sixty bucks on pizza, wine, and Oreos for his grumpy roommate last night," I retorted, tapping the combo for my locker in and opening the door. "I didn't even get any of the pizza. She squirreled it away into her room before she went to your place and spent the night with Brie."

He grunted.

"Still not talkin' to her, huh?"

He followed me out to the staircase to the lower floor. "We spoke this morning. She's going to her mom's tonight because her grandma's going over for dinner, so I guess we'll talk tomorrow."

"You guess you'll talk?" I snorted and pushed open the glass gym doors. "You've been together for two years. You've lived together for six months. And you're going to stop talking to each other because you were texting a woman you—actually, yeah, never mind. I think I might be on Brie's side here."

Sean groaned, shoving his hands in his pockets. "She assumed I was only texting her. I was texting my mom most of the time, and anyway, Georgia's texts were completely innocent. She'd forgotten to write down her hours, and I was talking her through logging into the employee portal."

"Did you tell Brie that?"

"While she was blind drunk? No. I fed her Advil and water and put her ass to bed." He shuddered. "The more pissed she got at me, the more she drank. I told her I was texting my mom, but she didn't listen."

"Why were you texting your mom?"

"My grandpa's in the hospital getting tests done. She didn't get back until late the other night. It's a three-hour drive either way, and she needed more clothes." He shrugged.

"And you didn't tell your long-term girlfriend that?"

He side-eyed me. "If I did, would I be here bitchin' about it to you?"

"You could try calling her and telling her, you know. It won't kill you."

"Yeah, but I don't know what's up with him yet."

"And you think keeping it a secret is going to make it better?"

He stopped on the sidewalk outside the restaurant. "Yeah? How's it going since you told Shelby you're in love with her?"

"I'm not in love with her," I ground out, shoving past

him to get into the restaurant. "I'm attracted to her and have unwelcome feelings for her, but it's not love."

Sean snorted. "Yeah, all right; I believe you."

I shook my head and went up to the counter, turning my attention to the menu like I didn't come in here every day when I was working.

He could believe what he wanted. He was keeping something important from his girlfriend—I was keeping inappropriate feelings from my best friend.

I had no desire to make things awkward with Shelby. There wasn't a chance she felt the same way about me, and we lived together.

Lived. Together.

I liked living with her. I liked what we had, even if she was going to bankrupt me with her love of Oreos. There were some things better left unsaid, and telling your best friend you had feelings for her was one of those things.

Nothing or nobody could change my mind about that.

Besides—I didn't want to tell her. I didn't need to. It was just a crush, an awareness of how fucking gorgeous she was now that we were together more than normal.

An awareness of my attraction to her, the conscious thoughts of how *badly* I was attracted to her, mixed with basic human lust.

Nothing more, nothing less.

If I told myself that, I had to believe it.

The last thing I wanted was for this to get any worse.

Especially since she knew what I looked like naked. Accident or not, the way her gaze had strolled all over my body before she'd screamed blue bloody murder said she'd taken a damn good look.

I didn't care. Her seeing me naked wasn't embarrassing for me, but I knew it would be for her. That was why I'd skirted on over it. I knew she'd had a good look; she knew she'd had a good look. Bringing it up would make it awkward.

And, honestly, I'd have a damn good look if I saw me naked for the first time, too.

Hell. I see myself naked every single day and still take a good browse of my abs every now and then.

It's good for the ego—mostly because I now live with a woman who doesn't think twice about bringing me down a peg or ten.

I placed my order, paid, and took a seat at the nearest empty table. Sean quickly followed behind me and put his receipt on the table next to mine.

"All right," he said. "So you're not in love with her. Fine. That I understand. We've all seen Shelby on a deadline."

My lips twitched. Deadline Shelby in public was a lot different to Deadline Shelby at home.

I still have nightmares from the time I woke up and found her rummaging in the fridge with her hair looking like she'd stuck her pinky finger in a power outlet.

I'd thought we were being robbed.

Nope. Just Shelby having a midnight snack and breaking the diet she swore she'd start on Monday.

Such was my life.

"But," Sean continued. "You live with her now. Do you really think that whatever this crush is is just going to disappear by itself? If you can make it beyond the Oreo and dry shampoo obsession and get the girl to shower daily during a deadline, she's a real catch."

I rubbed my mouth to hide my laughter. He did have a point—her showering habits during a deadline sometimes left some things to be desired, and if it happened with the next one, I already had her favorite deodorant in a box under my bed.

I planned on slipping it through her door with a packet of Oreos on day three.

Friendly reminder, sly dig… You pick.

"I don't know, man. It's probably just because we live together now and I'm seeing a different side of her."

"Even when she makes you do your own laundry?"

"It's a valuable skill. I even figured the dryer out all by myself."

"Don't tell Brie. She already has me vacuuming daily. I don't need any other chores."

"Really? You only vacuum? No wonder she gets pissed when you're on your phone."

He shook his head. "Don't fucking judge me. How many chores did you do until Shelby took your lazy ass in?"

We weren't going to discuss that. "Point is, I'm a changed man." I nodded at him as our food was brought over. I pulled my lettuce burger toward me, taking a second to look at it. The cheese was melted, the bacon was crispy, and the sweet potato fries on the side looked like I'd inhale them in two handfuls. "She's even drawing up a chores schedule. Something about making me into a man some poor woman will have to marry one day."

"That or she's trying to teach you to look after yourself for when she's finally able to get you to move out. Like when she gets a boyfriend." The look on his face was sly.

"Shut the fuck up and eat your lunch, or I'm putting you on bathroom cleaning duty this afternoon."

That wiped the smile off his face. He knew I wouldn't, but it drove home the point that I didn't want to talk about this right now.

I knew he was doing it to wind me up, but I wasn't going to fall for that shit. I was going to nip it in the bud before he took it too far.

I didn't care what he thought—I knew this crush was just that.

A fucking *crush*.

It'd pass, like so many of them had before and so many in the future would.

Screw the fact that if she'd walked into the bathroom five minutes earlier yesterday, she'd have seen me with my hand wrapped around my dick while thinking about her and hating myself.

She was my best friend.

My roommate.

I'd write it in graffiti on his bedroom wall and mine and hire a plane to fucking write it in the sky if that's what it took to make it clear.

No matter how badly I wanted to see if she tasted like Oreos and milk—I wouldn't.

Shelby Daniels was the one woman in this world who was off-limits to me.

Nothing could change that.

Nothing *would* change that.

The sky was darkening outside as I stepped out of the elevator on our floor and glanced out of the window. It overlooked the town, not the beach like the apartment windows had a glimpse of.

And it was just that—a glimpse. We had a sliver of a view between two buildings that housed apartments not dissimilar to ours.

Still, it was a "sea view" if you asked the realtors.

I hoisted my gym bag up onto my shoulder. I'd had a cardio class and two personal training sessions in the afternoon, and nobody wanted to be near a guy after that, so I'd showered and changed at work.

Mostly, I didn't want Shelby to accidentally walk in on me again because I'd forgotten to lock the door.

I stuck my key in the door and twisted it until I heard the satisfying sound of it clicking. The door edged open an inch, and when I pushed, the faint sound of music came from inside the apartment.

I couldn't place the song, but Shelby wasn't singing, so maybe it was new.

Trust me.

Nobody—and I mean *nobody*—needed to hear Shelby sing.

"Hello?" I called out, shutting the door behind me and dumping the bag with my dirty clothes. I'd put them in the laundry in the morning.

Hey—look at that. I was becoming an adult, finally.

"Jay, that you?" Shelby yelled from what sounded like her bedroom.

"Yes." I walked in her direction. "Is there another guy with a key I should know about?"

"Not that I know of." She appeared in her doorway with her hair tied back, held with a headband, and dark-green, shiny gloop on her face—one that brightened when she saw me. "Hi!"

I swallowed. "Do you know that your face is growing some form of algae?"

She looked at her fingers, two of which had a great big clump of it on, and the other hand that held a small pot with it in. "Oh! Facemask. I guess you've never seen me use it."

"No, and I'm not sure I *want* to see it."

"You should try it." She stuck her fingers out. "Your skin is dry. Let me make you pretty."

I took a step back. "My skin is fine, thank you, Dr. Pimple Popper."

"No. It's dry on your forehead. Come on; it's not that uncomfortable. I won't tell anyone." She advanced toward me.

"Shelby, if you put that shit on my face, so help me, I will smack your ass so hard you won't be able to sit down."

She waggled her eyebrows, smiling.

Or she tried to.

Whatever it was on her face, it was setting.

"You're turning into something resembling an ogre."

Before I could say another word to her, she darted out, quick as a bullet, and smeared her fingers down my cheek.

She laughed, trying not to move her jaw. "Got you!"

I smeared my fingers through the stuff on my cheek, my face crinkling in disgust. "Why would you do this? I don't need this shit on my face!"

"It'll make you pretty!" Her eyes shone with the laughter she wouldn't let her face express. "Now, come here and let me finish."

She dove her fingers into the pot and pulled out another clump.

"Nuh-uh. No way. You're not touching me with that shit!"

"Yes, I am!" She wiggled her fingers and chased me into the kitchen.

I gripped the edge of the island. "Shelby. No!"

"Come onnnnn," she pleaded. "Just one time. I won't tell anyone. What use is it living with your best friend if you don't do anything fun together?"

"We do lots of fun things together." I moved to the right as she slowly mirrored me. "We watch TV, we watch movies, we cook... You teach me about cleaning, and I pretend to listen."

She narrowed her eyes for a split second before she winced and put her expression back to normal. The paste was lightening now. "I won't complain at you for an entire day if you do this with me."

"Not good enough." I pointed a finger at her and carried on rounding the island, keeping pace with her. "You won't even be able to talk soon. Give it up, Shelbs. You're not putting the girly crap on my face."

"I am!" She launched herself at me with incredible speed, and once again, she caught me, but this time on the other cheek. "If you'd just—stand—still!"

The first cheek she'd hit was going hard, my skin feeling tight and uncomfortable. "Why does it feel like someone poured cement on my cheek?"

"It's supposed to feel like that," she said, her voice now a lot more muffled than before. "If you'd just let me finish—"

I laughed and walked back.

Right into the sofa.

I staggered back onto it, only having the arm of the sofa to steady myself with.

Her eyes glimmered with laughter, and I knew I was cornered.

She'd won.

She was going to put the fucking green gloop on my face.

Expertly balancing the pot in the hand where she already had that crap on her fingers, she used the other, clean hand to grab my shirt and hold me in place. She climbed onto the sofa next to me, on her knees, and pinned me in place with her fist.

"Sit still. I don't want to get it in your eyes," she ordered.

"This is the most ridiculous thing you've ever made me do. I should just hand in my man-card." I met her eyes. "Not to mention that I can still get away from you, given that you have the upper-body strength of a newborn giraffe."

She sniffed. "But you won't."

I quirked a brow at her.

Then moved.

Shelby squealed, moving faster than I thought possible once again, hooking one leg around my waist as I moved onto my side. We went down together, me twisting so I was lying on my back, and her straddling me.

Heat flushed through my veins at the feel of her thighs on either side of my waist and her hand flat on my chest.

She was sitting on top of me.

Right on top of my dick that was twitching like a fifteen-year-old's in front of a Playboy magazine.

I swallowed hard, and she froze, inhaling through a small hole in her now-cemented-in-place lips.

Something flashed in her eyes, something indiscernible, and her throat bobbed with her own swallow.

"Well," she said through her tight face. "This worked out well."

I didn't say a word as she sat up a little straighter, then scooped some of the facemask onto her fingers and smeared it across my forehead. I didn't say a word as her fucking bare thighs rubbed against my hips when her constant leaning forward and sitting back up made my shirt ride up.

It was taking all my self-control not to toss that goddamn pot at the fucking wall and kiss her. Taking everything I had to control my most base desires not to let my cock get as hard as it should have been right in that moment.

She was moving and wriggling, leaning left and right and back and forth as she smeared this stupid shit all over my face, and I let her because I was afraid that if she stopped, I'd grab her and do something I'd regret in ten minutes.

So I gritted my teeth and let her get on with it.

She didn't seem to be affected by the fact she was practically sitting right on top of my cock, so I wouldn't let her know that I was.

The woman was a menace.

If I wasn't careful, she'd be my downfall.

Maybe she already was, with her tight ass touching my thighs and her soft fingers rubbing green shit into my face and her brown eyes shining with laughter.

"There." She sat back, pressing herself right against my cock, and examined her handiwork.

My cock twitched, slowly hardening at the extra pressure on it. If she noticed, she didn't say anything, but her chest did rise and fall more sharply than it had been a second ago.

I think.

I was too busy trying not to get a fucking erection.

"See? That wasn't so bad, was it?" she said brightly.

Too brightly.

"Shelby," I ground out.

She slid her way down my body, making my nostrils flare, and got up. "I need to wash my hands. Be right back," she garbled out, her voice too high and her words all stringing together. "Be right back!" she repeated again, disappearing into the bathroom quicker than I could tell her to wait.

Pushing myself up from the sofa into a sitting position, I adjusted my pants. Thank God they were sweatpants because the second the bathroom door clicked shut a little too loudly, my cock sprang to life like it had a fucking switch on it.

I groaned, shutting my eyes.

With any luck, she hadn't felt the semi that'd been plaguing me for the last few minutes.

Given the fact she'd been sitting right on it, I doubted that was the case.

Fucking awesome.

CHAPTER 9

Do Not Think About Jay Naked

Shelby

I grabbed the towel to dry my hands and leaned against the door.

My entire body felt like it was on fire, especially my cheeks, and my heart was beating like mad. My exit from the living room had been obviously awkward, and that just made my cheeks burn hotter beneath the facemask.

It'd only been a joke.

I'd only planned on teasing him.

Then he'd fallen on the sofa, and I'd laughed, and he'd moved, and I'd—

Oh, God, it was all me. I'd hooked my leg around his body like he was a tree and I was a koala bear. Momentum had done the rest, and the next thing I knew, I was practically giving him a gentle dry-hump as he lay there and let me put this mask on his face.

He'd felt it, too, hadn't he?

Oh, God.

I needed to leave the country.

I couldn't live with knowing what my best friend's penis looked like when he was naked, never mind what it felt like as I rocked on him like a wave rocked a boat.

It was unintentional. A total accident. Yet it'd happened. A little twitch. Slowly getting harder until I moved off him as inconspicuously as possible, which for me, was about as inconspicuous as an avalanche.

This was a disaster.

All for some facemask.

What was I doing with my life?

I groaned, pressing the towel against my stomach. I'd just climbed my best friend like a tree, rocked on his cock like a boat, and plastered him in facemask like we were about to have a girls' night in.

Except he was a guy. Not a girl. And we weren't going to paint each other's toenails and whine about men over wine and snacks.

This was why I'd lived alone and did shit like this in private.

Not once had I *ever* accidentally rocked on Brie's genitals.

I pushed off the door and looked in the mirror. Even though I couldn't see the redness of my cheeks, I knew it was there. My eyes gave it away—they were bright and shining, and even if I couldn't see the embarrassment in them, I felt it.

All the way to my freaking pink-painted toes.

Ughhhh.

I took a deep breath and set my shoulders. Lord knew I couldn't set my face. The mask had done that for me. I couldn't even twitch my lips without being afraid it would crack.

Double ugh.

I pulled open the door and went back into the living room. Jay was sitting on the sofa, feet up on the coffee table, with a bottle of water in his hands—and a straw inside the bottle.

"What are you doing?" I asked, even though half of it sounded like gibberish.

He looked at me, his face covered in the same, half-cracked, light green mask that mine was. "'Inking," he replied. "'Ot you one, 'oo."

I looked at the bottle on the table with a straw poking out of it.

I sat down, taking the water with me, and forced myself to look at the TV. No matter how much I wanted to look at his crotch, I wouldn't.

Not today.

No, siree.

I was done with that nonsense today.

I didn't want him to know that I'd felt it. He had to know, sure. I mean, it was his cock. That didn't mean I wanted him to know that I knew. It wasn't exactly small, you know what I mean?

You weren't likely to miss his erection in a blackout, that's all I'm sayin'.

My cheeks burned. Why was I thinking about Jay's

crection? I was a strong, independent, relatively-slash-questionably successful twenty-five-year-old woman in the prime of my adult life. Surely, I'd grown up past thinking about penises in my spare time.

Well, you'd think.

Apparently, I hadn't. Especially not when said penis was attached to my best friend.

Damn it!

I needed an intervention of some kind.

Maybe a date?

Yes! A date! That was a good idea! A chance to think about someone else's penis. Let's be honest, it was more likely that I'd get to ride a stranger's disco stick than it was Jay's. It'd been a while, but riding cock was like riding a bike, wasn't it? You never forget how to do it? Skill for life and all that?

Man, I was gonna be so pissed if that turned out to be wrong the next time I got me some.

There would be a lot of people behind spam emails who'd get a piece of my mind if they'd been lying to me.

Ugh, no, I didn't want a date. Not with the idiots the dating apps always spat out at me. Not a single one of those had ever gone well, and that didn't even take into consideration the ones who did actually look like their picture.

I was sure most people my age met people to date in bars. The problem with that was that the only bar I ever went to belonged to my parents, and, well, people in general.

I was an introvert by nature. Bars were not a place for me.

Why would I drink around other people when I could drink at home without pants on?

Exactly.

"How long does this stay on for?" Jay asked, prodding at his cheek. "Is it supposed to feel like cement?"

"Fifteen minutes, and yes," I replied, grabbing the remote from the coffee table. I was not going to sit here and watch sports news. He could get that on his phone.

"I was watching that!" he eked out through his now-stony face.

I shrugged. "I wasn't."

"I thought we were compromising?"

I met his eyes. "We are. I'm not putting *The Big Bang Theory* on. Compromise."

"If you put *Friends* on, I swear to God..."

"I wasn't going to put *Friends* on! I was going to browse the guide, but now I might just to piss you off." I shuffled farther down on the sofa and put my feet on the coffee table.

"Why are you allowed to put your feet on the coffee table but you yell at me?"

"I'm wearing socks. Nobody wants your crusty man-feet on the table, Jay."

"I don't have crusty feet. I shower daily, unlike someone else." He slid his eyes toward me, and they flashed with amusement.

"I showered this morning after that stupid run, actually."

"You showered *because* you went on a run. Not that

what you did was running. It was more… lumbering."

I punched him in the thigh. "I do not lumber."

"You don't run, either." His lips twitched like he was trying to smirk, but the mask stopped him from being able to.

Thank God.

I didn't need to dry-hump him and see him smirk all in the same evening, thank you very much. God only knew what that would do to my sanity.

"Whatever. Just because we're not all super-fit freaks like you with a stupidly healthy diet and an actual exercise routine." I swung my feet from the table. "Come on. We can take these off now."

He followed me into the bathroom. "You don't even need a routine. You just need to eat something other than pizza and get off your ass once in a while."

"My job is dependent on me sitting on my ass."

"You can get standing desks now."

I tossed him a wet washcloth. "You know, you'd be a better friend if you sat down and pigged out once in a while. Then I'd look a little hotter standing next to you."

"If you want to look hotter, just wash your hair more than once a week."

"I'm thinking of rescinding that roommate agreement and kicking you out." I rinsed my cloth and continued cleaning the mask off my face. "You're a lot ruder now that you're on the lease."

His laughter bounced off the walls of the small room. "It's only rude because it's true."

"You don't have long hair. You have no idea how hard

it is to be a woman. If you had to wash and dry this hair on a daily basis, you'd stop washing it, too."

"Right. Yet you willingly put this fucking cement on your face."

I looked up. He'd barely gotten an inch of it off his face, despite the fact he'd clearly tried hard. I bit the inside of my cheek to stifle my laugh. My face was clear of it apart from a few rogue flecks around my hairline, and I reached up to clean those while Jay frowned at the washcloth.

"This is fucking ridiculous."

My laughter burst free from me, and I grabbed a towel to dry my face. "Oh, my God. It isn't hard. You just have to scrub it a little."

"I did!" He held out the cloth, clearly affronted.

"Not hard enough!" I took it from him and spun him so that he was resting against the sink. "This might be uncomfortable."

He grunted. "No more uncomfortable than the concrete sidewalk you've put on my face."

I shook my head, got the cloth wet again, and lifted it to his face.

The problem with this was that I was right in front of him, and my eyes had no other option than to examine every inch of his face.

Slowly, I scrubbed at his skin, pulling the mask away. Bits of it flaked off into the short stubble that coated his sharp jaw, and I had to reach up and wipe them away more than once, feeling the roughness of the tiny hairs as they rubbed against my fingertips and my palm.

It sent…*things*…firing through my body. Things I couldn't focus on when I was standing here, practically leaning against him, cleaning his face.

As I wiped facemask from his skin, getting stuck in, leaving his normally lightly-tanned skin red and a little raw.

His bright green eyes seemed focused on me, yet he never quite met my gaze. He was always focused on a part of me, but it was my nose, or my hair, or the dimple on my left cheek.

It was awkward. It was almost as if it toed the very edge of our friendship, but I swallowed and carried on cleaning the facemask off him.

My heart jumped inside my chest when he moved, shifting his weight to the other foot. It was so freaking stupid that such a small movement could elicit such a sudden response from my idiotic little heart.

He's your best friend, Shelby.

Give it up.

"Close your eyes," I said quietly. "So I can do your nose."

He shut his eyes, his thick, dark eyelashes casting shadows over his skin. It was horrible to ignore it, taking all the strength I had, but I managed it as I wiped and scrubbed the cloth over every inch of his handsome face.

I wanted to carry on.

I wanted to rinse the cloth, squeeze out the green stuff, bring the clean cloth back to his face and just clean it because I could.

But that was weird.

I was weird.

This was my best friend. This was Jay. This was the guy who'd checked out my dates and cornered the people who'd tried to take advantage of me. This was the guy who'd slotted into the big brother role so easily until he'd moved in and screwed everything up.

He was my best friend.

What was wrong with me?

Why did I want to jump him like he was a trampoline?

I wiped the final bit of mask from his face and swallowed hard, stepping back. "There. Done."

His eyes opened, flashing with something I couldn't place. "Thanks. I'm never doing that again."

"Yeah." I shrugged one shoulder in an attempt to be nonchalant. "Green isn't really your color."

Jay smirked, moving away from the sink. "It's not yours either, but it probably won't be the last time I come home and see you looking like a swamp monster."

I rolled my eyes, turning my back to him. My heart was still racing from being so close to him, and I didn't want him to see my flushed cheeks. I didn't want him to know how my body had reacted to him—twice.

There would be no coming back from it if he knew.

"You missed some on your face." He took a step closer to me and took the cloth, his fingers brushing mine. "Right here." He touched the side of my head, right near my hairline, and lifted the cloth to it.

Slowly, I drew in a deep breath, focusing on the tiny scar on his cheek that existed because he'd scratched when he'd had chicken pox as a kid. It was preferable to looking into his eyes as he cleaned a bit I'd apparently missed.

I could swear I'd gotten it all—I was no rookie at the old facemask, after all—so I didn't know what he was doing. Did he want to make this awkward? Could he tell that I was being awkward?

Why was I being awkward?

What was I doing with my life?

Oh, God. I was a bad adult.

"I can get it," I said quickly, taking the cloth and facing the sink before he could say another word.

I was right—there was no mask left on my face, so why…?

"I got it already," he said, just as quickly as I had. "*Ocean's Eleven* is starting soon. You want me to make some popcorn?"

I grabbed the towel to dry my face, then I shook my head. The last thing I needed was a cozy night on the sofa with him right now. "I have work to do. Sorry."

It wasn't a lie. I did have work to do. I had to start writing up the article and work on my book and check emails and—well, I'd find something, wouldn't I?

I'd write the phone book to avoid him at this point.

"Right. The people in your head shouting again?"

I jerked my head his way, expecting him to be snarky, but he was grinning. "Yes. And they're trying to figure out how to kill a man named Jay."

Laughing, he left the room. "Make it violent. If I'm going to be murdered, I want to go out in style."

"Good to know."

CHAPTER 10

No Dates In The Apartment

Jay

Thank fuck she said no.

That was the only thought that rushed through my mind as I dropped onto the sofa. I ran my fingers through my hair and blew out a long breath, hoping it took the tightness of my muscles with it.

I'd never been so weirded out yet so turned on at the same time in my life.

Facemask. Fucking facemask. She'd gotten me damn good, and in hindsight, I should have just let her put it on me.

She was always going to.

If I'd let her, we never would've ended up in that position on the sofa.

That precarious fucking position where it took everything in me not to let my dick get hard.

It twitched now as I thought about it. About her sitting snugly on top of me, legs on either side of my hips, leaning right over my body and plastering me with that fucking stupid cement.

Jesus.

Then she'd wiped it off my face.

Fuck me dead.

I was ready to grab her and kiss her, facemask be damned. She'd leaned right up against me, her body all but pressed against mine as she'd removed it. She was so gentle at first, not wanting to hurt me, then she'd scrubbed harder.

Her eyes had touched every part of my face. I would put money on that. She was so thorough, so methodical, so precise in everything she did.

And when she'd wiped flakes of it from my jaw…

I closed my eyes and took a deep breath in.

Her touch was so soft. A fleeting one, just strong enough to register and send a shiver down my spine.

The worst part was that it wasn't like it was the first time she'd touched me like that. No, she'd done it before. She'd teased me about my stubble for months now, coming up and scratching my chin when she thought it was getting too long. She'd grin and tug at the small hairs, somehow managing to get them between her fingers.

Then there was the time I shaved it right off and she'd stroked my chin and called me a babyface for four days until it came back properly.

Never once had her touching it felt like it had tonight.

I had to face facts. I had very real feelings for my best

THE Roommate AGREEMENT

friend, and that was one hell of a fucking problem. Nothing good ever came of falling for your best friend, but it looked like I had a one-way ticket to I'm-Fucked-Ville.

I didn't know what it said about me. Shelby was the weirdest person I knew—not necessarily personality-wise, but because she was such an enigma. One minute she was onto me about picking up my socks, and the next she was putting pencils into salads while muttering to herself.

She'd tell me to do something, then do it herself ten minutes later. She had no qualms about banging on the bathroom door and shouting at me while I was taking a shit. She'd bring me lunch then yell at me for something later that night.

She'd make me watch her stupid shows while talking to herself. I'd seen her burn food because she needed to write something down in a notebook that had to be done *right the hell now*. Heck, I'd come in from a night out and found her sitting at the kitchen island with her laptop open at two in the morning, typing furiously, because the people in her head only talked in the middle of the night.

Shit, it made her all the more perfect. She lived in her own little world that was largely in her head, but she wasn't ditzy or forgetful.

No.

Shelby Daniels was the sanest crazy person I knew, and I knew I was falling in love with her.

Slowly. It was a little more every day. Every time she looked at me or laughed or did something that someone else might find annoying, I fell a little deeper.

And that was not fucking good.

She was my best friend. She was my roommate. Dating her was out of the question. Telling her how I felt was the biggest mistake I'd ever make. I needed to get the fuck over this puppy love thing before it went too far.

I couldn't even tell anyone. Sean would take the piss out of me, and Brie was far more loyal to Shelby than she was me.

I didn't begrudge her that, for what it's worth. Girls would be girls. Their loyalties would always lie with one another, and that was fine. It was just a shame my best friend was such a fucking little shit.

I leaned forward and buried my head in my hands, slowly dragging my fingers through my hair.

Three months ago, moving in with Shelby had been the easy option. My building was being sold, and I was about to be homeless. She needed a roommate to help her pay rent, and I was right there. I didn't need a roommate since I earned good money thanks to my dad, but she'd needed someone.

I hadn't been perfect. I owned that. That was why we had this stupid roommate agreement. It was to draw lines and create boundaries and make sure we both knew where we stood.

I guess there was no such thing as an agreement that kept the heart in check.

Fuck.

Why'd she have to walk around in little bright pink shorts and no bra, huh? Why'd she have to make me want her?

Wait—no. It wasn't on her. She had the right to wear whatever the hell she wanted and using that as an excuse for my want to kiss her wasn't okay. I was attracted to her because she was fucking attractive, and that was all there was to it.

It wasn't her fault that I saw her in a different light now.

It was mine. It was on me, but that didn't mean I wasn't delighted that the roommate agreement stated that, like I had to wear pants, she had to wear a bra.

Equality and all that.

Fuck. I needed to do something to get her off my mind. Usually, working out was my escape from it all. It was the way I removed stress from my life, but that hadn't been working.

All it'd done was get me eyed up by women in the gym.

Not that it was a bad thing. I was a human after all, and I would be lying if I said I didn't like the attention. The problem was that none of them were an option for me— staff and clients were off-limits to me.

I ran the gym and I was the one who'd set those rules.

That didn't mean I didn't need a distraction.

And I did. One of the female kind. I needed someone who'd take my mind off Shelby for one night so I could reset and go back to normal. Back to seeing her as my best friend and nothing more.

Yes. That was it. I needed a reset.

I needed a date.

Pronto.

Sean: I think u lost ur mind, bro.

Me: I think I'm doing the right thing. I need a distraction & Shelby isn't it.

Sean: I told u that u were in love with her.

Me: Not in love with her. Just feeling shit I shouldn't.

Sean: So ur gonna go on a date, fuck this girl, and go back to the apartment u share with ur best friend and pretend like u didn't just screw someone to get over her?

Me: No, I'm gonna have dinner with her & go home.

Sean: Ur plan for getting over ur best friend is buying someone else dinner and not even getting so much as a handjob for ur troubles?

Sean: Don't u kno the best way to get over someone is to get under someone else?

Me: When have you ever had a one-night stand where you've been on the bottom?

Sean: Point.

Sean: But still, u should have sex with her.

Me: Shouldn't you be more concerned about fixing shit with Brie?

Sean: She's staying with her mom. Georgia texted me this morning and she lost it. But it's that time of the month so I let her go.

Me: You have the finesse of an elephant & you're giving me relationship advice? Fuck off, man. Fight for your girl before you judge me.

Sean: Hey, u texted me first. I was being a good friend. U wanna text Brie instead?

Me: At this point, I'm gonna take your girl for dinner instead.

Sean: Great. Her fave choc is Hersheys Cookies and Cream and don't mention sharks. They make her angry.

I put my phone face down on the coffee table and pinched my nose. He was hard work, but for all his nonchalant bullshit, I knew he was hurting that his relationship with Brie was on the rocks.

All because of the new girl I'd hired.

Fucking hell, I was making a hash of just about everything right now, wasn't I?

Now, I was sitting here in my living room, counting down the minutes until I had to have dinner with the cute girl I'd met in the gym earlier today. All I really wanted to do was cancel and call Brie and drag her out for my reservation instead.

I hadn't seen Shelby all day. I was scheduled for the later shift today, starting at eleven, and she'd left for the library before I'd even woken up. She'd come back before I had and locked herself in her room. I knew better than to disturb her when she was working, so I'd cooked her dinner and left it covered in the oven for her with a note.

Otherwise, she wouldn't eat.

I might not pick up my socks, but I could cook a chicken like a boss. Despite my efforts at cooking bacon that almost always turned out badly, I was good at just about everything else. Shelby didn't always like to admit it, but my omelets were better than hers, and I could cook meat better than her.

I knew she was avoiding me, and a part of me was okay with that. I wasn't entirely sure I wanted to see her right now either. Last night was still too fresh. Every time I thought about it, I was reminded about how close I'd come to kissing her when she'd been wiping my face.

Kissing her was not a good idea.

Nothing good ever came from kissing your best friend.

I didn't have a lot of evidence to back that up, mind you, but the thought of explaining myself after I'd done it was more than enough to convince me that it was terrible, terrible fucking idea.

So I did the only thing I could do. I got up, casting a glance toward Shelby's closed bedroom door, and left the apartment. My truck was parked outside the building next to her car, and I climbed into it, heading for the steakhouse I'd picked for the date.

Don't get me wrong. I wasn't against having a date. If anything, I needed one. I needed to be reminded that Shelby wasn't the only woman in the world.

I knew that. On a conscious level, I knew she wasn't the only woman who existed, but sometimes it felt that way. I guess that was what happened when you lived with the woman you had feelings for.

She was always there.

I groaned as I pulled into the parking lot. I was ten minutes early because my mom would kill me if she ever found out I'd kept a date waiting. I wasn't the best roommate, but I was a perfect gentleman.

Mostly.

I locked my truck and tugged at the collar of my shirt as I headed for the doors. It was inevitable in a small town, but I hoped like hell I didn't see anyone I knew.

Unfortunately for me, luck was not on my side, because the moment I stepped into the restaurant, I laid eyes on the two people you don't want to see when you're going on a date.

My parents.

"I'm going to need a different table," I said to the hostess right as my mom saw me. "I don't want to go on a date next to my parents."

The young girl's eyes widened as she looked at them. "Oh. I'm sorry. We can move you!"

"No, it's fine." My mom waved her hand. "We're nearly done anyway."

"Mother," I said, but she stopped me.

"Sit down, Jay."

Shooting the girl a smile, I sat.

My dad gave me a sympathetic smile. "Sorry, son. We really are almost done."

"It's fine." I grimaced. "It's not like it's a date or anything."

Mom's eyebrows shot up. "It's not a date? Why are you bringing a girl to a steakhouse if it's not a date?"

Dad sighed, pinching the bridge of his nose. "Sarcasm, honey. Sarcasm."

Mom's green eyes widened as realization hit. "Ohhh. Well, we'll disappear real quick. You didn't stop by this week, and your grandmother is wondering whether you're still alive or not."

"Given that we're having this conversation, I'm still alive," I replied dryly. "Tell Grams I'll come by this weekend on my day off."

She nodded. "Bring Shelby. She has the ingredients for her favorite dinner."

"Why is she making her favorite instead of mine?"

"Because unlike you, Shelby stopped by this morning with some flowers."

Here we go.

"Why did Shelby take her flowers?"

"The same reason she always does." Dad grinned, leaning back in the chair. "She wanted information. She's working on some article for the paper about a haunted hotel and Mom's stayed there before."

Of course. "I didn't know that."

"Do you pay any attention to her?" Mom scolded me. "You only live with her. It wouldn't kill you to take an interest in her."

Oh, I took an interest in her all right. Too much, it could be argued.

"She just didn't mention it," I settled on saying. "She's been in deadline mode. She's locked away in her room right now. I haven't even seen her today."

"You've left her locked in her room while you're out eating a fancy steak?"

"Dear God," Dad muttered, motioning for the bill.

I felt the same. "Yes, but I cooked her dinner and left her a note that it's in the oven to be warmed up. If I didn't, she'd end up just having toast."

"See? You raised a gentleman, honey," Dad said, putting his card into the leather wallet his server handed him. "Leave the boy alone. He's perfectly capable of having a date and looking out for his roommate at the same time."

"But not visiting his family," she pointed out. "Your mother called me hysterical this morning."

"She called you hysterical because there was a corn snake in the front yard," Dad said dryly. "And that was only because I ignored all her calls the second I heard the voicemail that *said* it was a corn snake."

I choked back a laugh. Grams hated snakes with a passion, and if she saw one, she'd rather burn the house down as opposed to just leaving the harmless little thing to pass on by. If it was a copperhead I could understand, but her

Yorkshire terrier viewed corn snakes as a toy.

Maybe that was it. She was afraid Alice would bring it inside and then she really would have to burn the house down.

"I'll see her tomorrow," I promised. "I'll stop by after work with her favorite cake and clear the entire yard of snakes, deadly or otherwise."

Mom nodded, apparently satisfied by my response.

Dad signed the receipt and took his card, handing the bill back to the server. "Right, let's go, Georgina. Jay doesn't want us here when his date arrives." He winked at me, and I smirked, whole-heartedly agreeing with him.

While I wasn't even entirely sure I wanted to be here, I knew I definitely did not want my mother here.

Mom came over, kissed my cheek, and let Dad lead her out of the restaurant. I looked around but the girl I'd met—whose name was escaping me again—wasn't here yet, so I pulled out my phone.

I had two messages, one from a number I didn't recognize. I opened it and read it, and it was from my date who said her Uber was stuck in traffic so she'd be late, and she included her name.

Tess.

Bingo.

Thank you, Tess.

I texted her back that it was fine and asked her what she wanted to drink, then opened the second message. It was from Shelby.

```
Shelby: Thanks for dinner. Did you
eat?
```

I'd just hit the button to respond when the blond-haired girl I'd met earlier today was led over to the table—a girl I now knew to be named Tess. Instead of replying to Shelby, I locked my phone, tucked it into my pocket, and stood to kiss Tess on the cheek.

And, hopefully, start getting rid of my pesky feelings for another woman.

CHAPTER 11

Everyone Is Responsible For Restocking The Coffee

Shelby

I rubbed my eyes and hit the button on the coffee machine with a yawn. The machine sputtered to life, and I froze.

I hadn't put the cup under there.

"Shit!" I yanked open the cupboard and grabbed the nearest cup to shove under the machine. It was emblazoned with the words 'I'm cute, but I cuss a little' which seemed fitting for this morning because I'd already cussed at least ten times.

I'd been awake less than thirty minutes.

The haunted hotel article was nearly done, mostly because I'd stayed up until three a.m. working on it. Now, it was seven-thirty, and the only reason I was awake was that I had a phone call with a potential ghostwriting client at eight-fifteen.

As soon as that was done, I was turning in the article and going the heck back to sleep.

"Morning!" Jay bounded into the kitchen with far too much energy for my liking.

I grunted and pulled my cup from the machine to get the milk. He wasn't wearing a shirt, and his gray sweatpants were hung low on his hips, but I was too tired to tell him to put some more clothes on.

"Ah, you got out of bed on the right side today, I see."

I shut the fridge and glared at him. "Shush. You're very loud."

He grinned, grabbing his own coffee cup. "Did you work or get drunk last night?"

I poured the milk into my cup. "Worked until three. Got a call soon." I took two big mouthfuls of coffee, not caring that it was steaming hot. "Heard you come in at around eleven. Where were you out so late?"

He leaned against the kitchen counter, crossing his legs at his ankles. His biceps flexed as he grabbed the edge of the countertop. "I had a date, then I met Sean for a beer."

My eyebrows shot up as I did my best to ignore the jealousy that punched me in the gut. "You had a date?"

"I can get them, you know."

"Never said you couldn't. I thought you'd sworn off women after the last girl you dated showed up at your door when you'd never given her your address."

"That was six months ago." He laughed and grabbed his coffee to put sugar in it. "It was just one date. I don't think I'll see her again."

Damn it. I was way too happy about that.

Stupid emotions.

Stupid feelings.

Stupid Shelby.

"Was it bad?" I perched on one of the stools at the island.

He shook his head. "Nah. I mean, it was bad when I got there and found the table was next to my freakin' parents."

I laughed, but my mouth was full of coffee and some of it went up my nose.

Jay smirked. "Elegant."

I coughed, pinching my nose, and motioned for him to go on.

"Thank you, by the way," he said, taking the bottle of milk from the island. "For going to see Grams yesterday. She wondered if I was dead, apparently."

I nodded. "She did. She wanted to know why you were such a heathen who didn't visit anymore. I told her you were learning to do your own laundry, and she laughed so hard I think she broke a rib."

He shot me a withering look. "Anyway, I'm headed over there after work to repent for being such a bad grandson and clear her yard of snakes."

"Corn snakes again?"

He nodded. "She thinks Alice will bring her a present again."

"I swear that dog is actually a cat in disguise."

"She does act like it." His lips twitched. "You've also been summoned for dinner. She's making your favorite because you brought her flowers and made me look bad."

"Ah, well, I've been taking Grams flowers and making you look bad for twenty years now." Even when we were kids, I'd make daisy chains in her backyard and leave them around her house for her. Now, it'd evolved into carnations every time I needed information for a newspaper article because Betsy Cooper was a walking library.

Also, she made the best cookies, and she always had some on hand.

Work was more fun with cookies.

"Yes, thank you for that," he said dryly, his bright green eyes twinkling with laughter. "Anyway, like I said, you've been summoned for dinner. I figure I'll head there straight from work, do whatever she needs doing around the house and in the yard, then come back to shower and we'll head to my parents' place together?"

I finished my coffee and got up to put the mug in my sink. "You phrase that like it's a question. As if I'm not coming when she's making her spaghetti. It's the best thing ever."

"I know, I was just checking if you wanted to ride together or not."

"Why would we take two cars? It's pointless. Plus, if you drive, I can drink with your mom and laugh at your baby pictures." I grinned, leaning on the island with my hands flat. "That's always fun."

"Depends what your definition of fun is," Jay said darkly. "You being drunk is rarely fun."

"I'm a great drunk, unlike Brie. I'm still a functioning human being capable of doing things."

"Shelby, the last time you had girls' night here, I came back to you mounting the broom and shouting, 'Onward, noble steed!'"

"I want to write paranormal. I was practicing broom mounting."

"Sure you were." He pulled his lips up on one side. "All right, fine. I'll drive so you can drink wine with my mother and pick out the baby photos to embarrass me with in front of my future girlfriend."

I clicked my tongue and winked, despite the idea of him having a future girlfriend being slightly repulsive to me.

I know. I had a problem. A big one. My feelings had quickly gone from wanting to tickle his pickle to wanting to wrap myself around him and growl at any woman who came near him who wasn't blood-related.

The worst part was that I couldn't even blame it on raging hormones. I was totally clear of shark week. Nope. This was just a regular old attraction to my best friend.

Ugh.

"See, this is why you're my best friend," I said, opening the fridge and pulling some pre-packaged mango out of it. "You drive me around so I can drink wine and make fun of you. If you'd leave my Oreos alone, you'd be the perfect guy."

Jay's eyebrows shot up. "Look, I've done my laundry twice this week and not eaten any of your Oreos. I'm already there."

"Yes, but you still have a pair of dirty socks under the coffee table." I pointed that way with the fork I'd just grabbed. "And I had to clean the sink before I could brush my teeth this morning because you shaved yesterday and didn't do it."

He opened his mouth to say something before quickly shutting it and getting a rueful expression on his face. "Ah, shit. I meant to do that, but there was a delivery I had to go down and sign for. Your delivery, actually." He pointed at the box on top of the coffee table. "I guess I got distracted after."

"Let me guess, that was the last time you used the bathroom?" I raised an eyebrow, spearing a square of the bright yellow fruit.

"Pretty much. I went to work, then I had my date."

"Well, at least you didn't bring her back here. If I wanted to hear people having sex, I'd be living with Brie and Sean." Who were now talking, if the text I woke up to from her was any indication.

Jay tapped two fingers to his temple. "It's in the agreement. I remembered. Besides—I wouldn't do that anyway. It's simple respect." He shrugged and leaned forward, pinching a bit of my fruit.

I shot him a glare. Nobody touched my mango. Much like nobody was allowed to my Oreos.

I liked food, okay? And I *didn't* like to share it.

"I appreciate it." I smiled at him. He had no idea how much I appreciated it, and I wasn't going to mention it. "When are you working?"

"Trying to get rid of me?" His eyes sparkled.

"No, but if you're at work, you aren't eating my food." I swatted his hand away as he just managed to grab another piece. "Jay! Cut it out!"

He shoved it into his mouth, grinning around it. "It's good."

"So buy your own, you thief!"

Shaking his head, he rounded the island, coming for my fruit. I dropped the fork and pulled the plastic container close to my chest, using my other hand to shield it from him.

"Jay. Cut it," I warned him, walking backward. "You're not stealing my fruit."

"Is there more mango?"

"No. I ate it all."

"See, this is how you feel about your Oreos. I like mango, too. Share it." He advanced on me, quickening his pace.

I clutched the container so hard the plastic bent, and the juice from the fruit splashed against my shirt, but since it was yesterday's, I didn't care. "Jay."

"Shelby." He grinned, and something decidedly wolf-ish and playful flashed in his eyes, making my stomach clench.

"Stop it."

"No." He made one final dart at me, and I jerked backward with a squeal right into the island.

The squeal quickly turned to a hiss of pain as the protruding corner of the island slammed into my hip. I doubled over, dropping the mango I'd literally hurt myself to protect, and clapped my hands over my now-throbbing hip.

"Shit, Shelbs!" Jay closed the final few inches of space between us and crouched down, his hands immediately going to mine. "I'm sorry. I was just messing with you."

"It's fine." I winced as I moved my hand. "It was an accident. Protecting food comes at a price."

"Yes, it's very admirable," he said dryly. "Let me take a look."

I slowly straightened and moved my hands away. God

freakin' damn it, it hurt like hell.

Jay reached over and pushed up my shirt, his fingers brushing across the bare skin of my stomach. Despite the pain I was in, I drew in a sharp but deep breath at the contact.

"Shit—am I hurting you?" He looked up at me with concern filling his gaze.

I shook my head, pressing my lips together firmly. I didn't trust myself to say anything else to him. My skin zinged where he was touching me, and a bolt of heat shot through me when he gently pulled down the waistband of my old, ratty fleece shorts.

His fingertips were soft as they brushed across my hip. "It's just a graze, but it looks like it's going to be one hell of a bruise for a few days."

I winced right as his thumb touched the really sore bit. "Great."

"I really am sorry, Shelbs."

I pulled down my shirt so he'd stop touching me and gave him a weak smile. "It's fine. It won't hurt for long, then I'll be okay. Hey—you have any of that freeze gel stuff? Will that help?"

He stood without moving back. There wasn't any space between us at all, and I swallowed the lump that was forming in my throat before it made me say something stupid.

For a writer, I wasn't all that good with actual words.

"I have a box of it in my closet," Jay said, his eyes searching my face. "Gel and spray, but your skin is broken. It's gonna sting if you put it on."

I wrinkled up my nose. "Maybe later?"

He smiled and nodded his head once. "Maybe try an ice-pack. You hit the counter pretty hard; the cold will bring out the bruising and reduce any swelling."

He stepped away from me to turn to the freezer, and I let go of a long breath. I was almost glad I was in pain. I could use it as an excuse for my reactions to him right now if it came to it.

"Here."

I blinked. Jay was standing right in front of me with a bag of frozen corn with a dishtowel wrapped around it.

"Put this on your hip," he instructed me. "Like fifteen minutes or so, okay? You can probably tuck it into your waistband."

"Right," I breathed, taking it from him. I almost dropped the bag and had to readjust the towel before I lifted my shirt to expose my side and did my best to put the bag in my waistband. The problem was, I couldn't hold my shirt, the waistband, and the bag at the same time. It was like juggling wet kittens.

"Let me help you." He came over again, extracting the bag from my hand. It took him all of ten seconds to secure the bag properly in my waistband while I held my shirt up. His fingers brushed my skin far too many times for me to be comfortable with such close proximity to him, but there was nothing I could do about it.

Jay took half a step back and met my eyes. "Better?"

I nodded, once again not trusting myself to speak.

"It'll help," he said. "At the very least, it'll numb the area and take away some of the pain you're feeling right now. Tonight, when the skin has healed up a little, I'll get the freeze gel, okay?"

More nodding from me. Like one of those little fuzzy dogs people used to put on the dashboards of their cars.

I missed those. They needed to come back into style.

"Shelbs? You okay?" Concern creased his brow.

"Yes. Sorry. It's cold." I smiled, but even I knew it was weak. The truth was, I'd really hit my hip hard, and I was a bit of a wimp about pain.

He lifted his hand as if he was going to reach for me, then froze as my phone vibrated on the island.

Shit.

My client call.

"I have to get that." My eyes widened and I half-walked, half-hobbled over to get it. The number flashed on the screen with a vague familiarity, and I dipped my head to answer, deliberately not looking at Jay as I headed to my room.

That was enough closeness for one day.

CHAPTER 12

Hair Does Not Belong In The Sink

Shelby

U nfortunately, that wasn't enough closeness.

In the debacle with my hip and then my work call, followed swiftly by a tasty two-hour nap, I'd forgotten all about agreeing to have dinner at Jay's parents.

I mean, great. That was what I wanted to do when my hip was still smarting and turning into a rainbow.

Not to mention that my new client had given me a slightly tighter deadline than I was used to. Never mind that she was paying me so much more in a rush fee that I didn't even need a roommate this month, it was still overwhelming.

I thrived under pressure. Unless the pressure was living with a man who I had a major crush on.

Then I didn't thrive.

Then I wanted to curl into a ball in my closet and hide

forever.

But that wasn't an option, because we had plans. Dinner with his family. Something I usually loved. Don't get me wrong, I loved spending time with my parents, and I had Brie's family, too, and her mom happened to be my mom's best friend, but there was something about Jay's family.

It was his grandmother.

Betsy Cooper was a delight. She stood at exactly five-foot-tall, but she wore three-inch heels to the grocery store and the butchers, had a violet streak in her otherwise bright-white hair, and wore the brightest pink lipstick you could imagine.

She could also drink a military guy under the table.

I wanted to be her when I was old.

Two knocks on my door pulled me out of my reverie. "Shelbs? You ready?"

I did a double-take at the gruff sound of Jay's voice. "Yeah. Two seconds. I just need to tie up my hair." I shut my laptop and got off my bed, moving toward my dresser. I grabbed two hairbands from the pot on the top and used the mirror to tame my dry-shampooed-to-fuck hair into a messy bun on top of my head.

I looked perfectly presentable in every other way, so I tugged up the waistband of my light-blue, ripped jeans, and readjusted my lemon-yellow shirt so it sat properly again. The jeans weren't so tight that they put pressure on my sore hip. Honestly, they were more like jeggings than anything.

And since I was a fan of leggings, jeggings were the next best thing.

I unlocked my bedroom door and stepped outside. Jay was leaning against the wall that divided the hall from the main living area, focused on his phone while he waited. His legs were crossed at his ankles, and his chin was almost at his chest as he typed furiously on his phone.

His black t-shirt hugged his lean, toned torso perfectly, and the dark-gray jeans he wore were just tight enough that they wrapped around his upper thighs without giving too much away.

It was unfair that he looked so fucking hot for a family dinner.

I hovered, clutching both my wallet and my phone in my hands until he looked up.

"Sorry. Sean's been texting me. I'm ready to kill him." He pocketed his phone and pushed off the wall. "You ready to go?"

"Yep." I followed him into the main room and pulled a light jacket off the hooks by the front door. "What's up with Sean?"

"Still fighting with Brie," he said, locking the door behind me and tossing his keys into the air only to catch them again. "I thought they'd made up this morning, but I guess something happened because he bitched his entire shift until I sent his whiny little ass home two hours early."

"Why was he bitching? She hasn't said anything to me. She said they were fine today."

Jay shrugged. "Maybe he was just bitching, then. I don't know. I think I tuned out around the time where he told me why women were the worst."

"Ugh. Women *are* the worst." I pulled open the door to his truck and climbed in.

"What?"

"Women are the worst," I repeated, grabbing my seatbelt and buckling in before I looked at her. "We're hard to live with, hard to understand, and even harder to get along with. We like to pretend that we support each other, but the fact is, most of us would sooner bitch about another woman and drag her down."

"That's some deep talk before a family dinner, Shelbs."

"It's true. And men aren't exactly great. We all have our faults. We could all do better as human beings."

"Great. You've gone from best friend to philosopher. Are you sure you write fiction and not those phony self-help books that are full of quotes pulled from random memes on the internet?"

"I don't spend any time on the internet," I said, staring out of the window.

"Liar. Last week, you told me you were writing, then when I checked in with you, you were taking a quiz on Buzzfeed to find out which Disney Princess you were."

I opened my mouth and closed it a couple times before my response came. "We all need a break when we work. I like to take stupid quizzes on the internet. You can't judge me."

"Oh, I can judge you, and I am." He laughed, hitting the stick so his blinker came on. "It's why I work with people. I like to judge them."

"I know. I've seen you watch *Big Brother*. You judge every single person on their walk into the house before you've even seen a real episode."

"Shelbs, if you go on reality television, you're literally inviting people to judge the fuck out of you. Kind of like when you're in deadline mode and open the door in last week's tank top, two-day-old sweats with a coffee stain on, no shoes, and pizza sauce around your mouth." He paused, changing gears. "And that's before anyone looks at your lack of washed hair."

"Look, personal hygiene isn't always a thing when I'm finishing books, okay? The voices can be loud. Kind of like a room full of toddlers."

"All right, but it wouldn't kill you to use a wet-wipe now and then."

I leaned over the cab and hit him in the arm. "You're a jerk."

"I know." He grinned, totally unbothered by my lame-ass punch. "It's why you love me."

I choked on my own spit, only just managing to wave him off by grabbing the bottle of water from the center console and rasping, "Dry throat."

He shrugged it off. "But seriously, Shelbs, the shower is your friend."

"And the vacuum is yours," I shot back, wiping the corner of my mouth. "Don't think I haven't noticed that you haven't even looked at it, much less plugged it in."

"Oh, but Shelbs—"

"You do it so I don't have to!" I said before he could.

I met his eyes and burst into laughter along with him. He was insufferable, but he was right, so… Who was I to argue with him?

I did do it. He really didn't have to. I needed to change that. Make a schedule for something. "Maybe we really do need a schedule for chores. Like making you do the vacuuming and sink cleaning once in a while."

"I don't know," Jay said slowly, pulling onto the streets where his parents lived. "A schedule? Would it work around work? Eh…"

"Stop trying to get out of it. It's the one thing we haven't properly addressed since the roommate agreement."

"Chores? A schedule? I'm going to tell you the same thing I told you the first time you mentioned this. We're not five, Shelby. I would think a pair of adults could figure it out." He parked behind his parents' cars, blocking them into the driveway.

I slid my gaze his way. "I just showed you the closet in the hall this week. Have you ever gone into it and used any of it to clean?"

"No, but—"

"That's why we need a cleaning schedule." I gave him a pointed look before I opened my door and jumped out. He did the same, and I said, "It'll make it easier to live with each other. Besides, I might be more apt to share my food with you if I didn't have to clean your man hair out of the sink."

"All right, but I'm not touching the drain in the bath. That's all on you, Rapunzel." He bopped me on the top of my bun, causing me to glare at him. "Fair is fair."

I rolled my eyes as he knocked twice on the door and pushed it open. "I never said I wouldn't do it. We did put it in the roommate agreement, you know, and it was my addition, not yours."

"Yeah, yeah, I know. I was just reminding you." His grin was playful. "It also means you're responsible for cleaning hair off the glass door of the shower."

"Cute. Mr. Can't-Work-The-Vacuum is making cleaning demands."

"I bet I could work the vacuum if I tried."

"Then try," I said dryly.

"At least he's doing his own laundry," another voice called from the kitchen. Betsy. She appeared in the doorway, grinning widely, her blue eyes sparkling with laughter. "I bet he used that internet thing to figure it out, though."

"Grams," Jay groaned.

"He didn't," I replied, walking over and kissing her on her powdered, wrinkly cheek. "He couldn't even turn it on until I talked him through it. Never mind that he forgot detergent."

Her drawn-on eyebrows shot up, and she looked around me at him. "You forgot detergent? What's wrong with you, boy? You're soft!"

I bit the inside of my cheek to stop myself laughing.

"I didn't think!" Jay protested. "Honestly, I knew this was a bad idea. I should have left when Shelby got out of the truck."

I rolled my eyes as the sound of his dad laughing filled the air.

"Shut up!" Jay shouted, sliding past me and his grandmother, but it only made his dad laugh harder. "The crap I get from the women in my life is bad enough without you adding to it!"

"That's why you're still single!" his dad shouted back.

I grinned. "No, his poor housekeeping skills and lack of ability to be a functioning adult is why he's single."

Jay shot me a look. "When did you last wash your

hair?"

"Washing my hair doesn't make me an adult. Using a vacuum cleaner and knowing which spray cleans the sink does. Spoiler alert: it's the one that says kitchen cleaner on the bottle."

"How did I know they were all different? They all look the same!"

Betsy sighed, shaking her head. "I don't know how you went so wrong, Jay." She dipped her head and winked at me. "Is it your father? Did I do a bad job with him? Lord knows it's not your mother. She's a delight."

"Who's a delight?" Georgina, Jay's mom, walked in with a wide smile and pulled me into a one-arm hug.

"We were just debating how Jay grew up to be such a bad adult and how much of a delight you are." I grinned, keeping my eyes on Jay. He narrowed his at me.

"Oh, well, in that case, carry on." Georgina squeezed me one last time and walked over to Jay, kissing his cheek. "Hello, darlin'. How was your date last night?"

"Jay had a date?" Betsy questioned. "Poor girl."

I clapped my hand over my mouth to stop myself from laughing.

Jay side-eyed his grandmother as she stirred spaghetti in a big pot on the stove. "It went well, Mom."

Georgina pulled a bottle of white wine from the fridge. "Are you seeing her again?"

"No."

"No?"

"No," Jay repeated.

"Why not?" His mom quirked one eyebrow as she poured three glasses out. "You just said it went well."

He sighed, rubbing his hand through his hair. "It did go well, but I don't see it going anywhere. She was nice enough, but yeah."

"Probably too nice to put up with your crap," Betsy said brightly.

"I cleared four perfectly safe snakes from your yard today and put up three shelves."

"Yes, and you had to be guilted into visiting me in the first place." She sniffed.

Jay looked at me. "Remind me again why I came?"

I shrugged, taking the glass Georgina handed to me. "You made me come. Don't look at me like that."

"You came because your mother said so," his dad shouted from the living room.

Jay muttered under this breath. None of us caught what he'd said, but that didn't stop Betsy jabbing her spoon at him through the air for his insolence.

The back door nudged itself open, and Alice announced herself with a tiny yip that made me grit my teeth. The Yorkshire Terrier and I had a tempestuous relationship, mostly because her so-called barking made me cringe, like nails on a chalkboard, and the damn creature knew about it.

The tiny dog trotted through the kitchen, stopping right in front of me. She looked up at me with big, black eyes before turning her back to me and trotting off into the living room.

I watched her as she went until the sound of Betsy

chuckling pulled me back into the kitchen. "What?"

"You'll get along one day," she said, dipping a tea-spoon into the spaghetti sauce to taste it.

"I doubt that," Jay said, stepping up behind her and peering over her shoulder. "She barely gets along with herself."

"Remember who sleeps in the room next to you, jack-ass," I shot back. "I'm also a writer. I could kill you and dispose of your body, and nobody would ever know."

"Ah, but if you did that, you'd never know the pleasure we'll get on his wedding day when we post the picture of him using a submarine as a pseudo-penis in the bathtub." Georgina grinned, her green eyes sparkling the same way Jay's did whenever he teased me.

Jay groaned, slumping against the counter. "Can we not?"

"Oh, but you were so cute!" she cooed, using her wine glass to hide her smile.

I sipped my wine to stop myself from smiling. Oh yeah. This was why I loved family dinner at the Cooper's.

It was the one night in my schedule where I didn't have to be the sole troll designed at getting under Jay's skin.

It was the best.

CHAPTER 13

The Liquor Cupboard Should Always Be Stocked

Jay

Tipsy Shelby was a fucking hoot.

Let that be noted. She was a total party after three glasses of wine, but tonight she'd had four. After the disaster that was Grams bringing out the old photo albums after dinner, Shelby had finally had enough wine to tip her over the edge of the stress she'd been holding tight in her shoulders the last few days.

Now, sadly, it was my job to get her into the elevator and into bed.

And I was stone-cold sober.

She was currently giggling in the passenger seat while looking at her phone. It could have been anything from cats jumping onto other items of furniture to people falling over or even the general news. She needed this downtime. She worked so hard for so little, so much for other people that I didn't begrudge her this giggly time at all.

She'd be fine when she woke up tomorrow.

Still, I had to get her out of this truck.

I pulled up into my usual parking space and glanced over at her. She was still giggling, and she typed as she did so. I frowned at her for a second before I got out of the truck and walked around to her side.

"All right, you, come here." I held out both of my hands for her to grab so she could jump down from the cab. "Let's go."

Shelby looked up from her phone, her eyes wide and ever-so-slightly glazed. "Are we at home?"

"We're home, Chardonnay-girl," I replied, gripping her wrists and guiding her down from the truck. "And you need to write tomorrow, so it's time for bed."

She jumped down from the truck, her flats silently hitting the sidewalk. "Really? It's bedtime?"

"Sure is. Mom and Grams opened a bottle too many tonight, huh?" I wrapped one arm around her body and held her against me, ignoring the way she seemed to slot against me like she was made for me.

"No, shush." She held one finger against her lips and burst into giggles. "I can walk, I promise. I'm not as drunk as Grams. I can handle an elevator."

I seriously doubted that. It took a hell of a lot to get my grandmother drunk, and she was nowhere near this tipsy when we left. "Well, just in case."

I selected the key on the ring with one hand and put in the code for the building, hauling Shelby in with me. She almost tripped on the tiny step inside, but she grabbed hold of my shirt, fisting the material, and giggled again.

I shook my head, wrapping my arm around her a little tighter, and pressed the button on the elevator.

Shelby hiccupped.

My family was a terrible influence on her.

"Water and aspirin when we get upstairs, okay?" I looked down at her.

She looked up at me with her brown eyes widening. "I'm not that drunk, Jay."

"You'll still thank me in the morning. I'll even make you breakfast."

"As long as it's not bacon," she muttered. "It's not normally possible, but you made bacon taste bad."

I rolled my eyes and guided her into the elevator. I wasn't going to argue with her on that—bacon was, for some reason, my nemesis in the kitchen—and I just didn't want to argue with her.

Arguing with her, in general, meant I would lose, and since alcohol made her more stubborn than usual…

Let's just say I wanted to do it as much as I wanted Wolverine to give me a prostate exam.

"You were a cute baby," Shelby whispered, cupping her hand over her mouth like we were in public. "Even when you used submarines as a penis."

"I didn't use submarines as a penis," I replied. "I happened to be holding it in that position when Mom took the photo."

"It's going on the wall at your wedding."

"I'm never getting married."

She groaned. "Birthdays, then. I'll send them to the

email of your future girlfriends. I will find a way!" She punched the air, almost sending herself toppling over.

"Not that drunk, my ass," I said, pulling her back before she could stumble through the now-open doors and fall flat on her face.

"I'm fine," she mumbled, once again gripping my t-shirt. "Got a bit excited."

"You're insane."

"No, I'm not. It's not my fault there are voices." She tapped the side of their head. "They're loud. One of them wants to have sex."

Jesus fucking Christ.

"Oh. That's my voice." She snorted then clapped her hand over her mouth to hide it.

My eyebrows shot up, and I stopped outside the front door to look down at her. "Your voice is the one who wants to have sex?"

Her cheeks flushed, and she refused to meet my eyes. "No comment."

I stared at her for a moment longer before I let her go to put the key into the lock. It clicked when I turned it, and I pushed the door wide open so I could easily help Shelby through.

"I got it." She waved her hand in my direction and used the doorframe to get inside. I shook my head, following her and shutting the door behind us. I paused to lock it, turning just in time to grab Shelby and reroute her to the kitchen.

"Water and aspirin," I reminded her. "I'm not going to listen to you complain about a hangover tomorrow just because you had a little too much wine with my mother. By now, you should really know better."

"Pish." She gripped the counter as she opened the fridge. "Your mom is fun. Especially when we get out the baby pictures."

"I'm going to call your mom and have her send me your baby photos."

"Go ahead. She probably lost them." Shelby looked over her shoulder at me. "You know what she's like. She can't even remember my birthday most years without setting herself a reminder."

Well, that was true. She was the ditsiest person I knew.

I pulled the aspirin from the cupboard and tapped two out of the bottle for her. I set them down on the wooden cutting board and got two for myself, then took hers over to her. She was frowning at the water bottle, and I grinned when I realized what she was doing.

I put down the pills again and took it from her, easily untwisting the cap.

Now, she frowned at me. "How did you do that?"

"I twisted it the right way."

"Ohhh." She tilted her head to the side. So much so that she almost fell over.

"Okay. Drink this and take the aspirin. You've had enough injuries for one day." I handed her back the bottle and shoved two of the pills at her.

She did as she was told, taking them from me. She tossed them into her mouth and washed them down before setting the bottle down. "Thank you. You're such a good friend. Even if the voices in my head want to have sex with you."

My eyebrows shot up as she sent me a dreamy smile. "All right. It's time for you to go to bed."

"Are you coming with me?" She giggled, clutching the water.

I rounded the island and gripped her upper arms to direct her to her room. She was clearly drunker than she was letting on, but that was what happened when you drank three glasses of wine before you ate dinner.

"Jay's taking me to bed." She giggled more, but this time, it was all interspersed with hiccups. "Oh, dear."

Oh, dear, was about right. That was exactly how I felt right about now.

"Here we are." I pushed open her bedroom door. It was so much tidier than mine was. I had clothes strewn across the floor where I'd tossed them into my laundry basket and missed, but there wasn't as much as a trailing cable on hers. Her desk didn't even have an empty glass on it, and there was already a coaster on the nightstand. Even her damn trash can was empty.

It was amazing how two such different people were such good friends.

"Can you get yourself changed?"

Shelby turned, eyes widening, and looked at me. "You want to undress me?"

Yes.

"No," I replied. "But I don't want you hurting yourself again if I leave you alone."

"Ummm." She looked around the room. "I think I'll be okay." She gave me a small smile.

"You sure?"

"Sure." Shelby turned her body toward me and touched her hand to my upper arm. "Thank you for putting up with my antics with your family."

My lips pulled to one side. "Yeah, you're making it hard for me to ever bring a girl home to them because I don't think anyone will compare to you."

She dipped her head, mouth curving slightly, and looked up at me through thick, dark eyelashes. "They have to get through me first anyway."

"Now that's the scary part."

She laughed, lightly swatting at my arm and swaying. She gripped my arm to keep herself upright. "Wow. Okay, maybe there was more wine than I thought."

It was my turn to chuckle. "You think, smartass? You sure you're good in here?"

She nodded resolutely, her bun bouncing on top of her head. "I'm good. Wait." She paused. "Yep, I'm good. Thank you."

"All right." I half-smiled. "See you in the morning."

"Night, Jay." She leaned over, and at that exact moment, I turned to go.

And her lips touched mine.

They were so soft, just like I'd imagined them to be. It was barely even a kiss, but my arm twitched because all I wanted to do was reach out, wrap my hand around the back of her neck, and pull her in close to me. I wanted to curve an arm around her waist and hold her body flush against mine so I could kiss her properly and thoroughly, make her feel the way I felt right now.

Like my veins were on fire.

Like nothing had ever felt this good.

But I couldn't. She'd been drinking, and she'd gone for my cheek—at least, I assumed she had.

So I went against every single instinct in my body and stepped away from her, letting her hand fall from my arm.

She instantly covered her mouth with her hand and blinked at me. "That wasn't supposed to happen."

I swallowed, ignoring the harsh thumping of my heart. "It's fine. You went for my cheek, I moved... It was an accident." I checked my Fitbit on my wrist for the time. "I have to go to bed. Work."

"Right, right." She pressed her hands against her stomach and took a couple of steps back. "Night, Jay."

"Night, Shelbs." I turned and hightailed it out of her room, making the sharp turn to my door that was only feet away from hers. I shut it behind me a lot more calmly than I felt and leaned against it.

Fuck.

She'd kissed me. By accident, but she'd still fucking kissed me. No matter how short and sweet and mistaken it was, there was no way I'd forget how it felt.

It was the longest three seconds of my life.

I rubbed my hand down my face and pushed off the door, then tore my shirt off over my head, tossing it in the direction of the laundry basket. It landed on the edge, mostly in, and I sat on the edge of the bed.

Going on a date with Tess last night had been the first step in my plan of getting rid of how I felt about Shelby, yet it'd ended up making everything worse. If I hadn't gone, I wouldn't have seen my parents, and I wouldn't have ended up at dinner with Shelby tonight.

She wouldn't have drunk wine with my mom and grandmother. She wouldn't have gotten drunk, and she wouldn't have accidentally kissed me.

Leaning forward, I buried my face in my hands and groaned.

This was a problem.

CHAPTER 14

Everyone Needs Their Own Space

Shelby

I was never drinking again.

I swear. That was a promise. It wasn't going to happen. Never, ever again, not after what I'd done last night.

I'd kissed Jay.

Freakin' kissed him.

Why had I gone in for the cheek? Why had I done something so silly? I never kissed his cheek. I'd only ever done it on birthdays and Christmas to say thank you for the presents. I'd never done it before bed.

What was wrong with me?

And I'd told him one of the voices wanted to have sex with him and that the voice was mine.

I was so glad he hadn't made me breakfast like he'd originally said. I couldn't begin to imagine the conversation.

Morning, Jay, I'm sorry for accidentally kissing you and telling you I wanted to have sex with you.

I rested my forehead against the fridge and groaned. My phone rang, and I reluctantly moved to get it. Brie's name flashed on the screen.

"Hey," I answered.

"Wow, what's wrong with you?" she said instantly.

"Nothing. What's up?"

"I just took lunch to Sean at the gym because I was out getting mine and Jay was miserable as hell. Sean said he'd been like it all morning. Do you know what's up with him?"

I groaned, sliding onto one of the island stools. "Me. It's me."

"What's you? What did you do? Did you finally have enough of him and tell him to move out?"

"No. I kissed him."

The sound of choking came down the line, followed by a big wheeze.

"Brie? Are you okay?"

"You kissed him?" she rasped after a second. "Why did you do that?"

"It was an accident!" I snapped.

"Whoa, okay," Brie said. "Calm down."

I took a deep breath and let it back out again. "You're right. I'm sorry. I'm just super stressed over it."

"Okay. What happened?"

"We went for dinner at his parents' last night. I had wine with his mom and Grams, and I was a little tipsier than I thought. He helped me into my room, and when I went to kiss his cheek goodnight, he turned, and I caught his lips."

"Oh, shit. That's not awkward at all."

"Yeah, well before that, I'd already told him that the voices inside my head wanted to have sex, but it wasn't a fictional voice, it was my voice."

"So you told your best friend you want to have sex and then kissed him. You're a mess, Shelby."

"I know." I slumped forward on the island, raking my fingers through my hair. "What do I do, Brie?"

"Why don't you just tell him how you feel?"

"No way. Last night can be written off because of the wine, but telling him I have feelings for him can't be ignored." I got back up and opened the fridge for the orange juice. "We have to live together. If I tell him I have feelings for him, it's going to be awkward. I know he doesn't feel that way about me."

"Do you? He's pretty damn moody. Just grunted at me when I said hi. Maybe he does have feelings for you."

I shook my head even though she couldn't see it. "He doesn't. It was weird after. If he had feelings, he wouldn't have pulled away, would he?"

"Maybe he pulled away because you were drinking and it was an accident."

"I don't know. I'm kinda hoping we can just forget it ever happened."

Brie blew out a breath that crackled down the line. "I don't know. You didn't see him today. I don't think forgetting is an option."

"But I want to forget."

"That's not how it works."

"I don't care. I want to forget it happened, so we're not going to talk about it."

"What if Jay wants to talk about it?"

"Then he can talk about it. It doesn't mean I'm going to reply."

She was silent for a moment. "You're hard work, do you know that?"

"I'm familiar with hard work. I washed my hair this morning. Drying it was a bitch." I paused. "I know you're right and that I have to talk to him about it, but I'm not going to admit that I have a crush on him."

"Fine. It's your funeral if he ever finds out you were lying, especially if he feels the same way."

"He doesn't feel the same."

"You don't know unless you ask."

"Brie, I love you, but that's the dumbest thing I've ever heard. If I'm not going to tell him I have a crush on him, then I'm not going to ask him if he has one on me."

I practically heard her rolling her eyes.

"Okay, okay. I get it. It's hard now that you're living together, but maybe you can't ignore this forever. And think about it—if he shares your feelings, you don't have to deal with the hoopla of moving in together."

"But if we ever broke up, we'd be living together."

"A slight complication," she admitted. "Just… Brush it off, then. Pretend it's no big deal, and eventually one of you will move on—probably him, since you only venture outside for food—and then you'll hate yourself for never telling him while he's marrying some hot other woman and you're cut out of his life, because a pretty, single female friend would be threatening to his new wife."

And we were done with this conversation.

"Bye, Brie." I hung up before she could say anything, and her text message that followed was very simple: **LOL.**

I knew I was being a little bit irrational over this. If Jay wasn't my best friend, this wouldn't be an issue, but I didn't want to complicate things. I didn't want to add another dimension to our friendship. Telling him I'd been crushing on him since he moved in wasn't exactly a good idea.

Despite what Brie said, I did have to face him at least once or twice a day. I didn't want him to be looking at me and wondering if I'd been fantasizing about him—or, hell, knowing Jay, he'd ask me outright just to get under my skin.

No. I'd made my choice. I'd talk to him about what happened last night, brushing it off as all mistakes. That was the easiest route to go down. Mostly because it wasn't exactly all lies.

It *was* an accident that I'd kissed him.

Never mind that I'd wanted to step in closer and wind my fingers in his shirt, prolonging it. It was still a mistake.

Mostly because I hadn't gotten the good ol' drunken sleep that comes after one too many glasses of wine. Nope. My brain had me tossing and turning all night with the memory of that one kiss.

More than once I'd woken up all hot and tangled in my sheets with my heart pounding. I couldn't remember the dreams, but I didn't actually need to.

The gentle throbbing between my legs had told me everything I'd needed to know.

All that from one kiss. One poxy little kiss that barely even counted as one in the first place.

It was ridiculous, quite frankly.

I glanced at my phone for the time. I didn't know what time Jay finished work, but if we were going to talk about what had happened, I was going to ply him with food. He could criticize my diet all he liked, but the way to that man's heart—and brain—literally was through his stomach.

So through his stomach I would go.

The sound of the shower running filled the apartment as I juggled the grocery bags in my arms. I had to kick the door shut behind me before I dropped the heavier bag of the two, and I still only just made it to the island before it dropped.

Phew.

That one held wine.

All right, I'm a big fat liar. But something told me I'd be grateful for it tonight, if only so I had something to do with my hands.

I unpacked the bags, laying everything out on the countertop. I had everything I needed to butter Jay up before we tackled the hard stuff.

I put the wine in the fridge and started on the rest of it,

leaving everything I needed out. By the time the shower stopped running, I'd sprayed and wiped down all the counters and swept the floor.

He'd either only just gotten in the shower when I got back, or he was taking a leaf out of my book and spending half an hour in there for no reason.

I hummed as I opened the kitchen closet and put the brush away. Then, on closing the door, I looked up.

Jay was standing in the bathroom door, eyes wide as he looked at me. He wore nothing but a black towel clutched around his waist, and much like the last time I'd seen him after a shower, water was dripping over every inch of his body.

I jerked my gaze away. I did not need to fantasize over him now.

"Shit, sorry, Shelbs. I didn't know you were back."

"It's fine." I swallowed and turned around. "I went to the store to get dinner."

"Oh. I thought you were out with Brie."

"Could you put some clothes on before we continue this conversation?"

"Fuck—yeah. Give me five minutes."

He could have all the minutes he wanted. The longer he stayed away, the more likely it was that my heart would be beating normally again when he came out.

Instead of thinking about him, I shuffled into the kitchen and got started on preparing the meal. Starting with the thin steaks, I pulled them out of the packaging and cut them into thin strips.

"Sorry," Jay said, drawing my attention over my shoulder.

He wore dark-gray sweat shorts and a white t-shirt.

"It's fine. At least it wasn't as bad as last time."

"True story."

"How was your day?" My voice went up an octave. Damn it, was I trying too hard to be normal? I was, wasn't I?

Introverts weren't designed for this kind of human interaction. We were more of a mumble and hide in a blanket-fort kind of people.

"It was all right. Yours?"

"Not bad." I swallowed, tossing the last of the steak strips into the pan. "Got some work done and took on another client."

"Awesome. What are you cooking?"

I felt the warmth of his body as he stepped up next to me and thank God I had to wipe off the board and knife in the sink several feet away from him.

"Is this Grams' carbonara recipe?"

I nodded as I cleaned off my things, not daring to look at him. I feared that if I did, I wouldn't be able to look away again. "I stopped by on the way to the store. She wrote it out for me." I half-heartedly pointed at the piece of paper on top of the mushrooms.

"You went there especially to get this?"

"No. I tried to get her spaghetti one, but she was having none of it. Hit me with this one instead and told me she'd leave the spaghetti to me in her will. I figured that was the best I was going to get."

Jay laughed, moving so that I could put the board back down again. "You're lucky she promised that. She swore to Mom once that she'd be buried with it."

"I'm sure it'll only be handed over with the demand I sign a non-disclosure."

"That sounds like Grams." He leaned against the island, gripping the edge of the counter with his hands. "So. If you're cooking my favorite, that means there's something wrong."

I filled another pan with water and set it to boil for the carbonara pasta. "Maybe I just wanted to do something nice for you."

"No."

"I can do nice things for people."

"Yes, but when you cook for them, it means you have bad news."

Sighing, I turned around. "It's not bad news, okay? I really did just want to do something nice for you. I wanted to... say sorry... for my behavior last night."

Jay smirked. "For getting drunk, telling me about the voice in your head wanting sex, and accidentally kissing me?"

I opened my mouth before closing it again and nodding once. "Yes. All of that."

He dipped his chin, laughing as he looked at the floor. "Shelby—"

"No, listen." I wiped my hands on a towel and held them up. "It was a mistake, and I'm sorry. I shouldn't have said what I did, and there was no need for me to go in and kiss your cheek anyway."

He peered up at me through dark eyelashes, his eyes flashing a stunning green, but didn't say anything.

"Now that's said, we can move on and forget it ever happened, okay?"

Jay clenched his jaw, but when he still remained silent, I sighed and turned around. If he wasn't going to talk to me, I couldn't talk to him.

Besides, I'd said my piece now. I'd apologized, explained, and moved on.

That was it. That was all that needed to happen.

I moved the recipe and tore into the mushrooms, grabbing a handful to put on the board. Jay still wasn't speaking, but I could feel his eyes boring into my back. He'd burn a hole through my chest if he carried on like that.

I shivered, uncomfortable with the scrutiny. Still, neither of us talked. Not as I put the pasta into boiling water or as I created the sauce or as I cooked the beef, onion, and mushrooms.

Jay just stood there, against the island, watching me.

It was unnerving. I didn't know what was going through his head, and I wanted to. Dear God, I wanted to know. I wanted to turn around and demand he say something, but every time I went to, the words got stuck in my throat.

I stirred the food until everything was done and I was able to drain the pasta and mix everything together. Serving it up, I glanced back at Jay. My eyes met his for the briefest second, and something about his intense gaze made my stomach flip.

Could Brie have been right? Was my crush mutual?

No—Jesus Christ, Shelby. That's ridiculous.

Don't even go there. That was a dangerous road to travel down.

I handed Jay his plate, and he uttered a quiet but tight "Thank you," and took his plate to the small, round dining table. I joined him, sitting on the opposite side.

The silence stretched as we ate. It wasn't the 'moving on' I'd hoped for, but hey, it was better than avoiding each other, right?

No.

It wasn't.

Silence was the worst.

The literal worst. I couldn't begin to guess what he was thinking. The tension in the air was crawling across my skin, making the hairs on my arms stand up, making me want to shiver until I shook it off.

This was horrible.

He was my best friend. There had never been anything we couldn't talk to each other about, and my stupid, tipsy actions had created something.

Ugh.

I glanced up at him, catching his eye for a brief second. He dropped his gaze the second our eyes connected, so I just sighed and got up to put my plate in the sink. I needed to empty the dishwasher, but I just wasn't in the mood right now.

I set to work clearing the dishes and wiping the sides down, trying to think of anything but what was happening.

Stupid wine. Stupid Shelby. Stupid brain.

Jay brought his plate over to the sink and put it in on top of mine. He paused, hovering behind me for a second.

The sound of him sighing filled the air, and just when I expected him to say something, he didn't.

He turned around and he walked away.

I'd had enough.

I slammed the wet cloth into the sink, splattering water over both me and the backsplash. Storming after him, I straightened my spine. "Jay."

He gripped his bedroom door handle, keeping his back to me.

"If you have something to say, say it."

"Nothing I have to say will be productive," he ground out, his shoulders visibly tightening.

Damn his tight t-shirts.

"But clearly you have something you need to get off your chest. If you don't want to share, then fine, but don't get on my back when I don't feel like talking to you, either." I turned away, heading back for the kitchen.

"Fuck," he muttered. "Fine."

I stopped and looked over my shoulder, raising my eyebrows in question.

He let go of the handle, slowly turning his body so that he could meet my eyes. "The only reason I stepped away from you last night is because you'd been drinking."

I drew in a short, sharp breath that quickly shuddered out of me. "What?"

"You'd been drinking," he said simply. "I…didn't want to be responsible for something you'd regret this morning, so I stepped away and left."

The lump in my throat was big. Suffocating, almost.

What was he saying?

"Are you saying you don't care that I kissed you?"

"I don't care that you kissed me." His eyes never wavered from mine. "But you do care, so it's a moot point."

"Right." I swallowed and wrapped my arms around my waist. "A moot point."

Except it wasn't. Nothing about any of this was moot. It was all very, very valid.

"Like you said, we can forget it ever happened and move on." Jay threw his arm out like he didn't care, but I could see otherwise.

The muscle in his jaw ticked. His biceps were taut, and there was a glint in his eye that told me he was lying.

More to the point, I knew he was.

I knew him. Better than I knew anyone. Better than I knew myself.

And I knew he was lying.

"You're lying," I said softly.

"No, I'm not."

"Yes, you are," I challenged, an edge to my voice. "Why are you lying to me?"

"Because you don't want to know the truth, Shelby. Trust me on that."

"If I didn't want to know, I wouldn't be standing here." I lifted my chin a little, defiance flaring inside me. "I'm your best friend, Jay. You can tell me anything."

"Not this."

"Yes, this."

He dipped his head, running his hand through his hair. "Fine. Fucking fine." He jerked his head back up and took a step toward me, fire flashing in his eyes. "I don't want to forget that you kissed me last night. I don't want to pretend like it never happened, because if you'd been stone-cold sober, I wouldn't have stopped you. I would have taken it a hell of a lot further and done something we'd both be regretting right now."

I felt like I couldn't breathe.

I knew the man standing in front of me, but I'd never seen this side of him. I'd never seen this... strong, almost darker side of him. I didn't know how to describe it, but I did know that my heart was beating soundly against my ribs and filling my ears with the frantic thud-thud-thud of my pulse.

"See?" He shrugged his shoulders. "Told you that you didn't want to know."

"Jay, I—"

He stepped out of my way when I reached for him. "Don't. Don't touch me, Shelbs, or this time I really will do something we'll regret."

CHAPTER 15

No Kissing Your Best Friend

Shelby

His words were a warning as much as they were a plea, but I didn't care.

We'd already crossed the line. At this point, our friendship was irrevocably changed. It didn't matter what we did.

So I swallowed the lump in my throat and dragged up some of the confidence I instilled in the heroines in my romance novels, and I closed the distance between us.

We weren't quite touching.

Not yet.

"Then do it," I whispered.

And grabbed his shirt.

He hesitated for all of a second before he framed my face with his hands, tilted my head back, and covered my lips with his.

Want pumped through my veins, filling my body with heat as Jay kissed me.

And it wasn't just a kiss. No—it was more than what last night's kiss had been. This was a kiss you felt in every inch of your body. My awareness of his lips moving against mine heightened each time he moved. Every kiss, every sweep of his lips, every inch closer our bodies moved together set me on fire.

I slid my arms up his body, wrapping them around his neck, moving onto my tiptoes to meet him properly. I fell back against the wall, but Jay came with me, never breaking the connection between us. His hands moved, one cupping the back of my neck and the other going to my waist, his fingers digging into my skin as my shirt rode up.

Tingles danced across my skin at the touch, and I whimpered into his mouth as his teeth grazed my lower lip. My clit ached, and my nipples were hard inside my bra as lust took me over.

At this point, I didn't care what happened. Not as long as he just didn't stop. I didn't want him to stop because I'd never wanted anything this much in my life.

I was so in trouble.

I'd never imagined that my best friend would be the one who'd have the power to break me.

As if he'd just had the same thought, Jay slowly pulled back, his lips resting at the corner of mine. "Shelby "

"I know." I dipped my head so his lips dragged across my cheek, leaving heat in their wake. His jaw brushed mine, the stubble making me shiver as it rubbed my skin. "This is a bad idea," I said softly.

He stiffened. "Yeah. You're right. It is."

Neither of us moved. My fingers stayed where they were, now wrapped up in the soft cotton of his t-shirt, and he didn't move his from my neck or my hip.

I shuddered out a breath. Jay rested his chin on top of my head when I sank down from being on my tiptoes. I pressed my face against his chest, taking a deep breath.

This was going wrong. So very wrong.

My eyes stung, and I extracted myself from his arms before he could see me cry. Everything I'd felt for long knotted into a ball in my chest, making it feel tight, and I managed to keep it compressed until I'd shut the bathroom door behind me and slid the lock across.

Running away right now wasn't the answer, I knew that, but staying there in his arms wasn't exactly a solution.

I needed to process what had just happened. I had to work through the knowledge that Jay had wanted to kiss me. That he didn't care that I'd kissed him. That I'd basically goaded him into kissing, only for him to give me a kiss that wouldn't be out of place in a movie about two idiot best friends who had feelings for each other.

Was that what this was? Two idiot best friends with feelings for each other instead of just one?

Or was it one who was thinking with her heart and another thinking with his dick?

Whatever it was, whatever was happening, was too much for me.

The tight ball of emotion in my chest gave way, exploding into silent tears that escaped my eyes and trailed down my cheeks. I buried my face in my hands and slid down the bathroom door until I was on the floor, back against the door, face in my hands, legs up to my chest.

And I cried, silently. I let out all the worry and fear and frustration I'd felt today. I let go of the stress of keeping how I felt to myself, of all the denial I'd put myself through the past couple of weeks.

I let go of the jealousy that'd stabbed me when he said he'd been on a date, of the jealousy for Brie and Sean who hadn't gone through any of this when they'd fallen in love with their best friend.

Mostly, I let go of the lies I'd been telling myself.

As the front door slammed shut somewhere behind me, I hugged my knees and really cried it all out, because now, the fear of the future was very, very real.

All the things Jay had told me when he'd moved in came flooding back. He'd told me it would only be three months. That I had to let him stay. That it would be fun, that we'd have the best time living together.

Not once had he ever told me that I'd fall for him.

And that was the problem.

That hurt more than anything else that could ever happen.

By falling for my best friend, I may have lost him.

And I didn't quite know what to do about that.

I woke the next morning after Jay had left. He'd left a note on the fridge that he'd gone to work and he'd stop by the store on the way home to get something for dinner and that I should text him if I had any ideas.

Instead of that, I packed up my laptop and notepads

and hightailed it over to Brie's. It was still early and not so hot in the day that I'd be a hot, sweaty mess when I made it to her apartment, so I walked.

The walk felt good. My cry last night had, unsurprisingly, been good for me. A weight had been lifted off my shoulders, but that didn't mean another hadn't replaced it.

Still, the walk helped. The smell of the sea as it crawled up the small beach and pounded against the thick bars that held up the pier swirled around me, and the gentle breeze that swept in from the sea and through my hair meant it'd be a hot mess within minutes, but I didn't care.

Ten minutes later, I arrived at Brie's apartment block. Jay and Sean often worked the same shift at the gym when they were there together, so unless Sean had a day off, I knew I'd be alone here.

I wasn't ready to talk to Jay yet.

Yes, yes, this wasn't very adult of me, I know that. But have you ever accidentally made out with someone you were living with who you weren't in a romantic relationship with?

Exactly. Don't judge me.

Besides—I would go home tonight. Just late. When he was asleep. And handle it tomorrow.

Not everyone is capable of handling adult situations there and then.

I was one of those people. I didn't handle emotional confrontation well. Anger? I had that down pat. I was a feisty little shit when you pissed me off, but I liked to let my emotions out in my books and deal with it after that.

Writing was a surprisingly good way of working through your feelings. While I knew that Jay and I had to

159

talk—hell, we had to be honest with each other, not just talk—I also didn't know how to start that conversation just yet.

I walked up the two flights of stairs to Brie and Sean's apartment and knocked on the door. There was no answer, so I knocked again, and there was still nothing.

Knowing Brie wouldn't care, I pulled my spare key from my purse and let myself in. Their apartment was only slightly smaller than mine, but that was because they didn't have an open-plan living space like I did.

Brie said she didn't want to have the smell of burned toast in her living room, and after Jay moved in and burned his, I understood.

Brie couldn't cook. At all. She was lucky Sean could— that was why they'd decided to live together. So Brie would exist on something other than ham sandwiches and take-out.

We were a weird little foursome.

I shut the door behind me and went into the living room. I waited for a second to make sure I was alone, and when I was sure nobody else was here, I set up on the sofa.

Minutes later, I had my headphones on, music playing, and my laptop open on my thighs. I stretched out on the sofa with my back to the door so I could look out at the ocean—Brie had sacrificed more space for an ocean view because she was a dreamer at heart.

I liked space, and besides, I had a whole three-foot of ocean view from my living room. Woot woot.

After I checked my emails, I settled down to open. I opened my word processor and hesitated before I clicked on my new client's document. I would hate myself next week for this, but right now, I needed to work on my own book.

I needed to get this emotion out, so it was time to rip apart the lives of some fake people.

Who said fiction couldn't mimic real life?

I skimmed the last chapter and set to work. The words flowed easily from my fingertips as I manufactured drama for my fledgling couple and tore them apart like a piece of paper.

It was therapeutic, and the more I wrote, the faster I wrote. I was in my own little world, lost to the fictional world I'd created and the hearts I'd sadistically broken.

This had meant to be a fun romantic comedy, but whatever. They could laugh later. Once they'd died a little inside.

See? Fiction was totally the same as real life.

I mean, I was a little dead inside right now.

I kept writing. I broke their hearts again with a blowout fight where she stormed out and went to the beach to scream and cry her frustrations away. I was a little jealous I hadn't thought to do that last night, the lucky bitch.

I sighed.

A shadow fell over my laptop, and I jerked my head up and screamed. It was only Sean, but holy hell—my heart was beating a mile a minute.

I tugged my headphones off and stared up at him. "You scared the hell out of me!"

"I've been here five minutes!" He laughed, moving my laptop bag so he could sit on the coffee table. "Noise-canceling headphones?"

EMMA HART

I nodded, pausing my music. "Sorry. I didn't mean to crash your apartment."

"Then why are you here?"

"All right, I totally meant to. Aren't you working today?"

"Shelby, it's one-thirty in the afternoon. I finished at one."

"It is?" My eyes bugged, and I checked the clock in the corner of my screen. "Well, shit. No wonder I'm hungry."

Sean's eyebrows shot up. "How long have you been here?"

"Since around nine."

"And why are you here?"

"Can I plead the Fifth?"

He smirked. "Come on. I'll make us lunch, and you can tell me what I already know."

I sighed, made sure my document was saved, and followed him into the kitchen.

Sean pulled the fixings for a BLT from the fridge and grabbed a frying pan for the bacon. "Shit hit the fan yesterday then, huh?" He glanced over his shoulder.

"That's one way of putting it." I sat at the small square dining table and rested my chin on my hand. "He told you everything?"

"After I threatened to call his dad and have him put on toilet cleaning duty," he said, referring to the threat they commonly used against each other. "It wasn't too hard to guess what had happened. Brie told me you'd accidentally kissed him, and since you live together, you had to address it one way or another."

"Yeah, well, we did." I fiddled with the edge of a dish-towel that was in front of me. "Except we made things worse."

"I don't reckon you did," he said, once again glancing back at me. "It's only awkward because you don't have any space between you, which is why you're here, right?"

"Yeah. I don't know what to say to him right now, so I figure it's easier to hide out here and deal with it tomorrow."

Sean turned and laughed, keeping half an eye on the bacon. "Is it really? I know you, Shelby. You overthink everything. There's only so much you can let out in your books."

I took a deep breath. I knew he was right, but that wasn't the point. "It was so easy for you and Brie. Why is this so hard?"

He smiled sympathetically at me. "Because, if you remember, Brie was your best friend and Jay was mine. We met because of the friendship you and Jay had. We became friends by default until I told her I wanted to date her—something I decided when we met in freshman year, by the way."

I sighed.

"You and Jay have a lot of history together. I had nothing to lose by asking Brie out except my sanity."

I laughed, pressing my hand to my mouth. "True. I don't know. I just feel like if something is meant to happen, it'd be a hell of a lot less complicated."

"Shelby, Brie spent four days being mad at me because a new coworker was asking me how the new treadmill worked because she'd forgotten." He flipped the bacon.

"Yes, she tried to talk casually, and I shut her down, but not before Brie lost her shit. Nothing about relationships is uncomplicated."

I shrugged, once again focusing on the dishtowel. "I just—I just need some space from him. I can't get that at home. He's like a dog with a bone."

"Weren't you the one who demanded he told you what he was thinking?"

"Yes."

"But he's the dog with a bone?"

"That's irrelevant." I sniffed. "It's hard. I've had these feelings for weeks now, and I guess I wanted to forget that he was my best friend for a few minutes. Does that make me a bad person?"

"No." Sean moved to slice lettuce and tomatoes. "It makes you a human with real feelings, but that also means you have to face the consequences of your actions."

"I know that. I do, honestly. I literally write books about people having to face them. Like I said, I just need some space. It's impossible at home, and my parents' bar is the first place he'll look for me if he wants to find me."

"And you think *here* is at the bottom of his list?" He smirked.

"No, but I'm going to play the best friend card here and ask you to keep it secret that I'm here."

"You want me to lie to him?"

"No. I want you to help me make Brie lie to him."

He laughed hard. "I won't tell him you're here, all right? If you need space, you need space. As long as you don't mind sharing the sofa so I can play FIFA."

That seemed like a fair deal.

"You have yourself a deal."

CHAPTER 16

Don't Think About Sex With Your Roommate

Jay

Working out was underrated.

The stress relief you could get from your feet slamming against a treadmill or lifting some weights or punching the ever-loving fucking shit out of a punching bag was incredible.

Georgia stood on the other side of the bag, holding it steady. I'd finished work an hour ago, but she'd volunteered to spot me when I was doing weights and come down here. I appreciated that she hadn't asked me what was on my mind, but I had a feeling that was going to change as soon as I stopped.

It wasn't that I didn't want to—no, wait. I didn't want to talk about it. I didn't want to talk to her about how I'd kissed my best friend and how it'd tormented me ever since.

How we'd actively avoided each other like we hadn't

known each other for twenty years.

I'd told Sean, but he knew everything anyway. He knew about my feelings for Shelby, but Georgia knew nothing. I didn't want to have to explain everything, because at this point, nothing could make me feel better.

I was pissed.

I was pissed that Shelby had brushed it off. I was pissed that I'd acted like a dick, that she'd pushed me, that I'd given in and kissed her when I should have walked away.

I was pissed that I wanted her so much.

And I was pissed that I was pissed about that.

It wasn't a crime to want her the way I did. It wasn't a crime to be unable to stop thinking about her, but it was inconvenient as fuck.

I'd been a moody bastard all day and a generally horrible person to be around. I'd spent most of it in the office clearing paperwork and sending membership renewal reminders just so I didn't have to interact with anyone.

I stepped back from the bag and wiped my forehead with my glove. "Thanks, Georgia. I appreciate it."

"You done now?" She stepped out around the bag.

I nodded, undoing the gloves and dropping them to the floor. I took the water she offered me with a muttered thank you and drank half of it in one gulp, then grabbed my towel from the bench at the side of the room.

"Are you all right?" She hesitantly joined me at the side of the busy room. "You haven't seemed yourself today."

"Just a bad day," I reassured her. "Thanks for spotting me earlier."

"It's my job." She smiled shyly.

I returned the smile, but it was tight.

"Jay, are you sure you're okay? Is there anything I can do to help?"

Lifting my head, I shrugged and met her eyes. "I dunno. You ever kissed your best friend?"

Her mouth formed a little 'O.' "Oh, I, um—no. I mean, I don't swing—neither does she."

For the first time all day, I burst out laughing. "Your straight, male best friend."

"Ohhh." Her cheeks burned bright red. "Sorry. I just assumed—well, this is awkward."

"Don't worry about it." My lips twitched.

"So you kissed your best friend who's a girl?"

"Unless she changed sex overnight, yep."

"I can see how that would be a problem." She pulled her lip into her mouth and dragged her teeth over it.

I watched her do it and felt…nothing. Not even a twinge of attraction to the pretty girl who was sitting next to me. Absolute zilch.

I was in deep shit right now.

"I guess you're moodier than a girl on her period because you haven't spoken to each other since it happened?"

"You're good." I looked straight ahead at the people who were using the bags. "We live together, so it's even worse."

"Oh, snap." She scratched her chin. "That's definitely hard. Huh. What happened? Was it an accident? Like a drunken kiss? Or do you have feelings for her?"

"We weren't drunk." I decided not to complicate the story. "We had a bit of an issue, and I ended up kissing her. It was two-sided, for what it's worth, and it's because of my feelings for her that it happened."

"How long have you known each other?"

"Twenty years."

"Wow. Okay. That's a long time."

Slowly, I nodded. "Makes it harder, you know? It would be easier to brush it under the rug to protect our friendship, but I don't know if I can now."

"Do you really like her like...real feelings? Something worth acting on?

"I think I'm scared to admit the truth to myself, honestly, but I think so, yeah. It hasn't fucking gone away, I know that much."

Georgia leaned against the wall and blew out a breath. "Can I give you some advice?"

I waved for her to go on. "I wouldn't be talking to you if it was unwelcome."

"Right. Jay?" She touched my arm so I would look at her. "I don't know her, but if it were me and someone I really cared about had feelings for me, I'd want to know. Secrets can be more destructive than the truth. If she doesn't feel the same as you, you can both move on, even if that means you moving out, but you'll know. You'll be able to put it behind you."

"I guess I know that."

"*Does* she have feelings for you?"

"Not a clue. She's not exactly the easiest person to talk to about emotion. She's an introvert—the only thing she can express with any kind of accuracy is sarcasm." I snorted, dropping my eyes, only to sigh again. "And her frustration at my socks not being in the laundry basket."

Georgia laughed. "Well, you're the one who knows her, but even if she doesn't tell you, you have to tell her. I mean, from my perspective—if you like her, you have to go and make sure she knows that, even if she shies away from you. I'm not the best with emotion either, and we can thank my ex for that, but I'd still want someone to march in and demand we talk like something out of a romance novel."

I groaned. "She writes those. There's no way I could compete with the schtick she writes."

More laughter. "Then go read one of her books and, literally, take a page out of her book."

It was my turn to chuckle. I reached over and patted her knee. "Thanks, Georgia. I feel better now. I'm gonna go shower and see if I can hunt her down."

She smiled. "Good luck. I expect an update tomorrow."

I saluted her as I stood, then left to shower, my mind a little clearer than it had been before.

The apartment was empty when I returned. It felt eerily empty, like it'd been this way for hours. I dumped my gym bag down by the front door and checked the apartment room-by-room.

Her stuff was still in place in her room, so at least I knew she hadn't done a runner.

A hot shower at work had convinced me that I needed

to talk to Shelby, and it had to be now. She needed to know that the only reason I'd said her name yesterday was because I wanted more, not for her to cut it off.

She needed to know that I had real feelings for her, ones that rocked me and confused me every single time I set fucking eyes on her. She had to know that this wasn't a joke, that there was something more than friendship here.

At least from my side.

And I wasn't going to stop looking for her until I found her.

I quickly changed into a clean pair of jeans and a t-shirt, then grabbed my phone and keys to start Mission Find Shelby.

My first stop was the library. She would sometimes work there for hours because it was quiet and nobody would bother her. I pulled into the lot and rushed inside, only to be scolded by the librarian, old Mrs. Henderson, for not walking in an orderly manner.

"I'm sorry, ma'am," I said as I approached her desk. "Have you seen Shelby today?"

Her blue eyes glittered. "That's quite all right, Jay, but keep it in mind." She winked. "And no, I haven't. Been a few days since she's been in here, I reckon. Is everything okay?"

"Yes, no worries. Thanks, Mrs. Henderson."

"If she pops in this afternoon, I'll let her know you're looking for her."

"Thank you." I smiled and left, getting back into my truck and driving the few blocks to her favorite coffee shop. I had the same result there—she hadn't been in, nobody had seen her, and they'd let her know I was looking for her, and yes, everything was fine, thank you very much.

I tried a few other places on the front where I knew she liked to work, including the bakery and the café that made her favorite sandwiches.

It didn't escape my notice that the first few places I checked were centered around books and food.

If that didn't sum Shelby up, I didn't know what else would. It'd be on her tombstone one day.

Here lies Shelby Daniels, lover of books, food expert, and sarcasm connoisseur.

I shook that off and pulled up at the back of her parents' bar. It wasn't girls' night, so this was a long shot, but sometimes she came here when she needed to escape. The stories of some of the punters were often jotted down into the notes on her phone, especially during tourist seasons.

According to Shelby, everyone had a life story that was worth writing. At least in their opinion—hers was a lot different. She thought they were all tooting their own horns, but that didn't mean she didn't always get some juicy bits.

The bar was quiet as I'd expected it to be, and her mom was behind the bar drying some glasses.

Her face lit up when she saw me. "Jay, darlin'! How are you doing?"

"I'm doing good, Lucy, thanks. You?"

"Can't complain." She smiled, and her face lit up the same way Shelby's did.

Fuck. I'd be seeing her face in oil spills next.

"What can I get you?"

"Have you seen Shelby?" I leaned against the bar. "I can't find her."

She raised her eyebrows. "You sure she ain't holed up in a basement somewhere finishing a book? You know she turns into a hermit crab on a deadline."

"Deadline week was last week. I don't need air freshener anymore."

Lucy laughed. "Sorry, darlin', not seen her today. You tried calling her?"

"Ah, if only. She's avoiding me, so she won't answer even if I did."

"Stubborn thing. I can't imagine where she gets it."

"Me either," came the dry tone of Shelby's dad as he joined the conversation. He leaned over the bar and clapped me on the shoulder. "What's up, son?"

"Looking for Shelby. Have you seen her?"

He shook his head. "Sorry, Jay. Not today. You do something wrong?"

"The jury is still out," I said dryly. "I just need to talk to her. I'll call when I find her."

"You finally telling her you're head over heels in love with her?" Lucy teased me, her eyes saying she knew more than she was letting on.

I smirked, tapping the side of my nose. "Well don't tell everyone, Lucy!"

She laughed, jumping when Tom slapped her ass. "Woman, leave them alone and do something useful."

Tom winked at me, and I left, shaking my head. I stepped to the side on the sidewalk and pulled my phone out to call Shelby on the off-chance she'd answer. I wouldn't be that lucky because I knew she'd have her head buried in the sand right now, but I had to try.

Before I could, I had a message from Brie.

Brie: …What did you do?

I frowned and hit the reply box.

Me: What are you talking about?

I only had to wait a minute for her reply.

Brie: Sean got home from work and found Shelby camped out on our sofa. What did you do?

Shit. Of course. So fucking obvious. Why hadn't I thought of their place?

Me: She was at yours? Is she still there?

Brie: Let me find out.

I tapped my foot as I stared at the screen, willing her to text again. It felt like forever until her name popped up once more.

Brie: Sean said yes. What did you do?

Me: Tell him I'm on my way.

Brie: I'll meet you there, then, since nobody will tell me. Hmph.

I pocketed my keys and tore off toward my truck.
Bingo.

CHAPTER 17

Seriously, Personal Space Is A Thing

Shelby

hree loud knocks hammered on the door and Sean paused his game. He got up and stepped over my legs since my feet were resting on the coffee table and went to answer it.

I hummed along to "Sucker" by The Jonas Brothers as I typed. It'd been a nice afternoon, actually. My noise-canceling headphones had blocked out Sean's shouting at the idiots he was playing some shooting game with, and he'd only side-eyed me three times for singing out loud.

It was an introvert's match made in heaven. Socializing without talking. Perfect.

Until it wasn't.

My headphones were pulled off my head, making me wince as my ears almost went with them. "Hey! What the—" My protest died on my tongue as my eyes found the green ones that belonged to the perpetrator.

175

Jay.

I licked my lips and turned to Sean, putting my computer on the table. "You said you wouldn't tell him I was here!"

Jay's eyebrows shot up, and he looked at Sean.

He took a step back, holding his hands in the air. "I didn't tell him a thing, Shelbs, I swear."

"Then who did?"

"Me!" Brie wheezed as she stumbled against the doorframe of the living room. "Phew. That was quite the run."

"You told her?" I rounded on Sean. "You know I want some space!"

"What's—hoo," Brie breathed. "What's going on?"

I covered my face with my hands. "Great. Apparently, personal space doesn't exist anymore!"

"Hold on." Brie held up a finger as Jay worked his jaw in frustration. "I get the impression I wasn't supposed to tell Jay you were here."

"Ya think?" I was almost shouting now.

"Deep breath, Shelby," Sean said.

I took a deep breath all right, making sure he got the full extent of my annoyance in my glare.

"What is going on?" Brie demanded now that she had her breath back. "Will someone tell me why I was apparently harboring my best friend in my apartment before I ratted her out?"

I looked at the carpet, saying nothing. When Jay didn't say anything either, Sean sighed.

"They kissed last night, and Shelby is here hiding out

so she doesn't have to face up to what happened."

My jaw dropped. "I'm here to think!"

"For the love of God," Jay said, finally wading into the conversation. "Shelbs, this is ridiculous. We need to talk. Come home so we can."

"I just wanted some space." I turned to look at him. "We don't have that at home. I wanted to think without worrying I'd say something stupid. I'm still not at that point."

"You can't hide here forever. We're going to talk about this, and we're going to do it today."

I stood and put my hands on my hips. "Oh, we are, are we?"

Jay squared up to me and gripped my chin in his hand. "Yes. Because you have three choices. One: come home nicely. Two: I carry you out of here on my shoulder with you kicking and screaming. Or three: we do it right here, right now, and everyone will know just how badly I want to fuck you."

Well.

That was quite the turn of events.

"Three!" Brie piped up. "Pick—"

Sean cut her off by clamping his hand over her mouth, and I was very grateful for that.

"You wouldn't dare carry me out of here." I batted his hand away from my chin. "I'm not a child or a ragdoll."

"I don't care. We're going to talk about this right now. You're the one who stood in front of me last night and told me that I could tell you anything. You can tell me anything, and you're going to, just like I will you. But you're leaving this apartment with me, one way or another." His bright green gaze never budged.

A part of me wanted to see if he'd actually haul me over his shoulder. Or if he'd have the talk here.

But I wasn't that petty.

All right, I was a little bit petty, but I had no desire to be hauled over his shoulder like I was being saved from a burning building, nor did I want to talk about what had happened in front of our friends.

I glared at him for a moment longer before I turned and packed up my laptop. I heard Brie's "Awwww," of despair, the nosy little shit, but I ignored it as I moved deliberately slowly.

Jay clicked his tongue.

I took my sweet-ass time wrapping my cord around my headphones.

He sighed. If he thought that was going to make me move any faster, then maybe he didn't know me as well as I thought he did.

In fact, he was probably being as petty as I was.

After another minute, I put my phone into my purse and stood up. I shot him the widest, sweetest grin in my arsenal, and he clenched his jaw, but his lips twitched in response.

He wasn't very good at staying mad at me.

I was far better at being the one to hold a grudge.

I stalked toward the door, and when he hadn't moved, I turned, my hair flicking over my shoulder. "Well? Are you coming?"

"He hopes so," Brie piped up.

Sean replaced the hand over her mouth. "Sorry."

Jay took a deep breath and, with a shake of his head, followed me to the door. He stayed behind me the whole way down the stairs, and the only reason I had to wait was because I assumed he had his truck and I didn't have a car.

And me starting to walk would just start another war of words.

"Get in," he grunted, pushing the button to unlock it.

"A gentleman would open the door for me."

"My inner gentleman is busy. He's thinking about tossing you on the backseat and doing unspeakable things to you."

"My inner lady is responding by flipping you off." I yanked open the door and climbed up. I went to close the door, but Jay was standing there, and he smirked right before he slammed it shut.

He was such a jerk when he was all riled up.

Mind you, I wasn't exactly a nice person.

The drive was made in complete silence. We didn't even look at each other. It was weird. We always laughed and joked whenever we rode together, but this kind of felt like I was riding to my doom.

Dramatic, I know, but you don't write books without the taste for a little drama.

He pulled into the parking lot next to my car. I jumped out before he'd even killed the engine, and I made my way to the elevator and up to the apartment before him.

I put my laptop bag and purse on the armchair and readied myself for him to come up. Feet apart, hands on hips—I adopted the universal battle stance for a woman ready to unleash some sass on a man.

Jay didn't bat an eyelid when he saw me. Instead, he ignored me completely and walked right past me.

All right, so it wasn't as scary as I thought it was.

Or maybe *I* just wasn't that scary.

Probably the latter. I knew I always shit my pants a little whenever I walked in and saw my mom with her hands on her hips.

Jay said nothing, now bustling toward the coffee machine. He pulled a mug down and set the machine alive, still ignoring me.

Was this how annoying I was in Brie's apartment?

Wait, no. He wasn't allowed to do this. He was the one who'd stormed in there, interrupted me mid-sex-scene, and demanded we come home to talk.

Well, we were home, and he was making a fucking coffee.

"Well?" I said. "Aren't you going to tell me how you're going to fuck me seven ways to Sunday?"

Jay didn't respond.

"Are you still thinking them up? I have to admit; I thought you'd have them written down. Like a prepared speech or something."

Still nothing.

"'Cause now I'm a little curious. I mean, you already mentioned the backseat. One out of ten for originality on that, by the way. Pretty sure everyone did that in high school in some awkward dimly-lit parking lot. Not that I'd know since I stayed a virgin in school, but Brie did enough for the both of us."

His shoulder twitched.

Ah. I was going to have to wind him up until he just came out with it.

"I have to admit, you really got me thinking about all the places you could have sex and all the ways you can do it. I'm just throwing this out there: butt stuff is off the menu. That is a one-way system, thank you very much."

He cricked his neck to the side. Damn it. I thought the mention of butt stuff would do it.

I perched on the arm of the sofa. "So have you really thought about this or are you blowing smoke up my ass? I'm not a fan of that either, for what it's worth. One-way street and all that. Are you a doggy-style guy or a missionary? Cowgirl? Sideways missionary? Dang, there's a whole slew of them, isn't there? I don't think I even know more sex positions than that."

His upper body rose then fell.

I was breaking him.

"Although, now I'm starting to think you were just talking shit. You dragged me home so you could tell me how badly you want to fuck me, but here I am, still waiting, thinking up my own scenarios, yet you haven't said a word."

He gripped the edge of the counter.

"I guess that was just a threat to bring me home. It was a bad one, as far as threats go. You should have threatened to throw out my laptop or ban my TV shows." I tapped my finger against my lips. "Especially the laptop. That's a real threat." I shuddered. "My poor baby."

"Jesus Christ, Shelby, do you ever shut up?" Jay turned, jaw clenched and pinned me with his gaze.

I held out my hands and shrugged, pouting out my lower lip. "You're the one who said we needed to talk. I was just getting it started. It's not my fault you can't carry through with your threat of telling me how bad you want to fuck me, or were you just being a big burly alpha male because we weren't alone?"

"You wanna know? Really?"

"Are you gonna write me a note? Because my characters were in the middle of banging each other when you so rudely interrupted me. It was a bit inconvenient if it was all for nothing."

"All for nothing? Here's an idea—shut up, and I'll start the conversation by showing you just how much I want you."

"You have to keep your pants on, remember? That's part of the room—" I finished on a squeal. He'd closed the distance between us in seconds and with his hands under my arms, he tossed me backward on the sofa.

I bounced on the soft cushions, but there was no chance of me finishing my sentence. Jay leaned over me, sliding his body between my legs, and kissed me. I melted easily into the kiss, easing my hands up over his shoulders.

I hadn't aimed for this, but I can't say I was mad about it.

He kissed me firmly and deeply, his tongue teasing the seam of my mouth before he flicked it against mine. I whimpered at the feel of his cock hardening against me, and my fingers twitched where they were gripping his shoulders.

Every time he moved, just the slightest jerk, his cock pressed harder and harder at the seam of my shorts.

He ran one of his large hands up and down my thigh, his fingers just skirting beneath my shorts before he pulled them back and gripped my ass, pushing himself harder against me.

My breath caught between kisses, and he smiled against me. I didn't have to look to know it was a cocky, self-assured one.

He'd wanted to tell me, but he was doing one better.

He was showing me.

I still didn't understand. I didn't understand entirely why he was kissing me as passionately as he was or why he was so hard for me, but it was okay. Any reason he gave for doing it in this moment was a-okay with me.

Because, for the first time in my life, I felt the kind of magic I'd only ever written about.

I wanted to drown in this moment. To sink into him, into the kiss, and never come back up for air.

I wanted to wrap myself around him like a cocoon and stay there, holding him against me, so he could do nothing but kiss me.

And finally, finally, I knew what it was really like to be *kissed*. To be kissed so deeply and so real that you felt it down to your soul.

That's what kissing Jay was like.

The most real kiss I'd ever experienced.

With my best friend.

Holy shit. I was shamelessly making out with—and rubbing my clitoris against—my best friend and his rock-hard cock.

I couldn't help it.

I burst out laughing.

It made Jay pause and pull back, looking down at me with curiosity in his eyes. "That's the first time that's ever happened."

I clapped both hands over my mouth, doing my best to stem the giggles, but I couldn't. This day had been such a rollercoaster, and I didn't know if this laughter was simply nerves or because I was *making out with my best friend.*

Jay sighed, pushing himself upright. I scooted back from him so I could sit, too, and dipped my head until I had myself under control.

As much as I could, that was. I mean, my clitoris was throbbing like nobody's business. If it got much worse, I'd need a doctor. Or an orgasm.

Unfortunately, if I kept laughing, I didn't think an orgasm was likely.

"I'm sorry," I whispered behind my fingers, the laughter finally subsiding. "I just—I realized it was you I was making out with and I couldn't control it. Hell, I just rubbed myself against you like a bear rubbing against a tree."

"That's the strangest euphemism for dry-humping I've ever heard." He blinked at me. "And, like I said, never been laughed at during a make-out session before."

"It's not—shit. It's not you. I mean, it is, but it isn't. Not your kissing. You're very good at that. And, you know, it's not too shabby feeling down there either." I pointed directly at his erection before I snatched my hand back.

Why did I do that?

Jay was still looking at me with confusion, but there was a hefty amount of amusement mixing with it now, too.

Oh, God, I needed to talk myself out of this.

"You're my best friend. And that's a sizeable tree in your pants."

Scratch that. I needed to stop talking.

Jay ran his tongue over his lower lip. "I am familiar with the size of my penis."

"Good, good."

Why did I say that?

Jesus, I was so bad with words for someone who used them for a living.

"I mean—" I hesitated. "I don't think I know where I'm going with this if I'm honest. I think I'm just talking for the sake of it."

"You think?"

"Yeah." I let go of a shuddery breath. "Can you talk instead?"

His lips quirked to one side. "Nah. I'm quite enjoying you doing this. It's an improvement on earlier."

I groaned, pressing my face into my hands. My chin and jaw were sore from the stubble that dotted his, and my lips were swollen and tender, but no matter how awkward it was, I wanted to remember this. I wanted to remember what it felt like for him to kiss me the way he had.

Just in case he didn't want to kiss my awkward little ass ever again.

"You done?" Amusement laced his tone.

Wait, was he laughing?

I dropped my hands. He was. He was fucking laughing at me.

"Don't laugh at me!" I leaned forward and swatted his arm.

He rubbed his mouth. "Sorry. You're adorable when you get all tied up like that. It was fun."

I glared at him and folded my arms across my chest. "Shut up."

He grinned.

"You wanted to talk to me, so talk to me. And, for the record, I understand how badly you want to have sex with me."

"If only," he muttered. "All right. Listen to me for once, okay?"

I nodded once.

"I spoke to Georgia today—"

"Oh, good, there's nothing like being the subject of conversation between your best friend and a total stranger."

"You literally just said you'd shut up."

"You should have known better than to believe me."

Jay leaned over and pressed one finger against my lips. "Shut up and let me talk."

"What if I don't?" I mumbled against his finger.

He brought his nose just inches from me. "Then I'll kiss you until you can't talk anymore."

That seemed like a fair warning.

I batted his hand away. "Fine. Get on with it."

"I spoke to her briefly about this situation. And no, I didn't go into details, and since you don't go to the gym, you're not likely to meet her."

I pursed my lips.

His eyes glinted in the light. "She made me realize that best friends or not, there's a big conversation that we need to have. It doesn't matter what the outcome is, but it needs to happen."

"Way to scare a girl."

"Shush!" Jay laughed, reaching out and tugging a lock of my hair. "For fuck's sake, Shelby. Just shut up for a second!"

"Fine." I rolled my eyes. "Can you get to the point, though? I'm squirrelly today."

"Just today?"

"Shut it."

He rubbed his hand over his face, chuckling. "All right." He dropped his hand and met my eyes. "I'm going to be serious now. You think you can manage that for a couple minutes?"

"This is emotional, isn't it? Jesus, no, Jay—you know this makes me speak without thinking. What are you—"

He cut me off with a swift kiss, his hand curling around the back of my neck.

Okay.

So that worked.

He pulled back, his eyes boring into mine, but he never let go of me. "No matter what I'm about to tell you, remember this: you're my best friend. I don't want you to be anything but honest with me, okay? You won't hurt my feelings. You won't change anything. Keeping you in my life as my best friend is more important than anything. You understand?"

My heart was beating double-time. He'd already bypassed my comfort level when it came to emotional discussions. He knew it as well as I did because he kept his eyes on mine as I tried to control my breathing.

"Okay," I whispered.

CHAPTER 18

No Loud Noises After Nine P.M.

Shelby

It wasn't okay.

I wasn't okay.

Emotional stuff was something I'd always struggled with, and that was part of the reason I'd never tried to tell Jay how I felt.

I could put it on paper. I could fictionalize love and romance and crushes and everything else that came from having a passion for penning romance novels.

I just wasn't very good at verbalizing it.

It was why I'd never had a relationship last past six months in my life.

But now—this was Jay. He knew I didn't do this. He knew it made me uncomfortable, but he'd asked me to listen. So I'd listen.

Jay reached over and pushed some of my hair from my

eyes. I dropped my gaze, and I heard his breathy chuckle.

"At least you're listening," he said softly. "Shelbs, I have feelings for you."

I jerked my gaze back up to him. "What?"

He took a deep breath in. "I have feelings for you. Beyond friendship."

What. Was. Happening?

"Okay," I breathed.

He searched my face for a moment before he continued. "They're relatively new. Since I moved in, actually, and I wasn't going to act on them. I had no plans to change our friendship. You're the most important person in the world to me, Shelby. Losing your friendship would hurt me more than anything else."

Swallowing hard, I nodded my agreement as I dropped my gaze again. That was why I hadn't told him, wasn't it?

The idea of losing him was too much to bear.

It would kill me.

"But I have to tell you how I feel. If I don't, it's gonna eat me up inside. Even if you tell me I'm crazy—I have to be honest."

Okay. *Now* my heart was going crazy.

"I have real feelings for you. I want more than friendship with you. I want to take you on a date. I want to be more than your best friend."

Slowly, I met his gaze. Gone was the confident, playful, sometimes-cocky man I called my best friend. He'd stripped himself bare, and I could see nothing but honesty shining back from his stupidly green eyes.

He'd picked up his heart, put it on a silver platter, and handed it to me.

But I couldn't speak. My own heart was wedged firmly in my throat. I couldn't form the words I wanted to say, because there was only one thing I really needed to know.

Wanted to know.

"If you feel that way," I said in a scratchy voice. "Why did you take someone else on a date the other night?"

Shame flashed in his eyes. "I met her at the gym. I wanted to stop feeling this way about you. I took her out because I thought it would help me forget how I feel about you."

"Do you want to forget how you feel about me?"

"No." He reached for me before he dropped his hand. "No, Shelbs, I don't. Even if you tell me I'm stupid and our friendship is more important, I don't want to forget."

I brought one shoulder up toward my face and turned away, looking at the coffee table. It held an old coffee cup, two empty glasses, and a Pop-Tart wrapper I knew didn't belong to me.

It made my lips twitch.

"You need to learn to hide your junk food wrappers," I said absently.

"If I were anyone else, I'd be offended by that deflection."

"Not a deflection. An observation." I focused on it as I spoke. "Would you really risk our friendship for the chance of something more?"

"Honestly, I already have."

My head bobbed in agreement. "You know this is hard

for me, right? My instinct right now is to get up and lock myself in my room where you can't find me. I want to run away."

"I know."

"I want to hide and pretend this conversation isn't happening."

"I know."

"I'd rather write you a letter."

From the corner of my eye, I saw his lips twitch.

"I know."

"Because I feel the same."

He stilled. "You feel the same?"

I nodded jerkily. "Everything you said, I feel the same. And it scares me because nothing scares me more than losing you as my best friend. You've been there for as long as I can remember, and I don't want to lose that."

"Shelby."

I swallowed.

Jay framed my face with his hands. I turned away, so he moved, dropping to the floor, moving to where he could look into my eyes instead. "Nothing has to change," he said with a small smile. "We don't have to do anything about this. I can go stay with my parents instead. We don't ever have to be anything other than best friends, you know that, right?"

"I do," I whispered.

"Good." He stroked his thumbs across my cheeks. "I will never make you do anything you don't want to do. Except unclog the drain in the bathtub."

My lips twitched, and when I glanced up, my gaze got stuck on his.

He'd not only served me his heart on a silver platter, but it looked awfully like he'd offered me his soul, too.

Reaching up, I laid my hand over his on my cheek. His palm was so rough yet smooth at the same time. Like he used moisturizer right after he lifted weights as heavy as I was.

I kind of wanted to nuzzle against it like a kitten and ask if he'd pet me.

"Sleep on it," he suggested. "Sleep on this conversation, and we'll revisit in the morning. I'm not at work until midday. Georgia is opening for the first time tomorrow with Oli."

"Okay," I replied, even though I knew I wouldn't sleep a wink.

"Just don't make pancakes, okay? Actually, if you're friend-zoning me, make them. Then make them to warn me. But can you make them before I come into the kitchen so I know what to expect?"

Despite the emotion hurtling through my body, I couldn't help but laugh.

"Deal."

Let it be known that Shelby Daniels was a troll.

That's right. I was going to own the fuck out of that label as I mixed chocolate-chip pancake batter.

I figured turnabout was fair play. Jay had made me talk

emotions, so now I was going to get my own back, Shelby-style.

"Dancing with a Stranger" by Sam Smith and Normani was bursting from my phone, and I sang along and twirled through the kitchen to the beat. Which was, actually, a lot of hip swaying like I was freakin' Shakira.

Sometime around two in the morning, I'd made my choice.

If I didn't try now, I'd forever hate myself. If I didn't tell Jay that it was worth pursuing something, I'd forever be plagued with thoughts of what-if.

I hated those.

They were often the basis of my plots but in real life? Not a fan.

We had to figure it out, though. It wouldn't be easy. We lived together. Our friendship was important. But what could one date hurt?

It couldn't.

I tossed one pancake onto the stack and poured another, swaying from side to side.

"Oh, shit, I smell pancakes."

I grinned, dipping my head so he couldn't see. "Good morning."

"Is it?" Jay said warily.

I peered over my shoulder as the pancake batter bubbled. His hair was sticking up at all angles, and he wore his uniform lazy outfit: sweat shorts and a t-shirt. He had the look of someone who'd just woken up and come running to the kitchen.

"The sun is shining. There's a bird outside who finally

stopped singing when I did, and I'm making pancakes. Is there anything bad about this morning?"

"Well, you're making pancakes. Also, you're singing. That's not good at any point of the day. Especially not the shower."

My lips twisted. "You've never heard you singing in the shower, clearly."

"Hey—I'm a regular Ed Sheeran in the shower. I can sing the fuck out of 'Shape Of You.'"

"No." I shook my head. "You can't. Unless you'd like to drown cats and compare your voice, that is."

He grunted. "You're making pancakes."

"Yes."

"I know what that means."

"You forgot to put your Pop-Tart wrapper in the trash?"

"Bad news," he said.

"I don't know. If you think I ran to the store at seven a.m. for chocolate syrup and berries for bad news, well, maybe you've put the news on."

"Should I have?"

I put the latest pancake on the stack. "Not in my experience. It's never good when I look."

"I can't decide if you're trying to let a guy down gently or if you're trolling the fuck out of me."

I shrugged and poured another pancake. "Figure it out."

"If I could, I would."

Another shrug. "Eh."

I flipped the pancake. It landed perfectly in the pan, and I grabbed my phone. I changed the song to "Shape of You" and grinned at Jay. "Sing, monkey, sing."

He laughed, coming over to the coffee machine. "Only in the shower. It doesn't sound the same outside of it."

"Aw, damn. I thought there'd be some kind of entertainment for breakfast."

"All right, I'm starting to think you're trolling me."

I flipped the final pancake onto the stack and turned off the stove. I carried it over to the island and came back for the toppings. Jay joined me, carrying two coffees, and set one in front of me.

"Thanks." I smiled and took three pancakes for my plate, leaving him five.

His eyebrows shot up. "If you're leaving me an extra pancake, I know it's bad news."

"Shut up and eat." I grabbed the chocolate syrup and drizzled it over my pancakes, then took some of the sliced bananas, strawberries, and raspberries.

"There's an order I can live with." He did the same, piling his plate with the cut fruit before he drizzled basically half the bottle of syrup over his plate.

I side-eyed it for a second before going back to my breakfast.

Really. And he said I was the one with the bad diet.

There was more sugar on his plate than in the candy aisle at Target.

And I knew because I was a fan of that aisle.

We ate in relative silence, only occasionally glancing at each other. My phone circled through music in the background while the dishwasher whirred and the fridge buzzed.

And it was so, so comfortable.

And not because I was used to it. It just was. It was comfortable and...well, comfortable.

It felt right. To sit in silence and eat with him like this, even if he was full of nervous energy.

I had to put him out of his misery soon.

I swiped a slice of banana through the syrup and put it into my mouth before settling down my cutlery. Jay was still making his way through his, although he was going at warp-speed compared to me.

I didn't know how he could eat so much.

Standing up, I put the last of my breakfast into the trash and took the plate to the sink. No sooner had I rinsed mine off than Jay groaned and held his stomach.

"If it's bad news," he said, turning to me. "It was worth it."

"Good to know you value food over me." I swiped the plate from in front of him and put it straight into the bubbly hot water in the sink.

I felt the warmth of his body before I felt his physical touch.

He came up behind me, trapping me against the sink with his body. It was awfully bold for someone who thought what I had to say was bad news, but I digress.

"What are you doing?" I asked, amused.

"Trapping you until you give me what I want."

"Are you out of coffee?"

"Don't sass me, Shelby."

"Aw, you're taking away my very DNA."

He dipped his head, his lips brushing across the bare skin of my neck. My hair was currently looped on top of my head, but his breath sent loose tendrils fluttering over my skin.

"All right, stop it!" I turned, pushing him away. "Stop that!"

He grinned.

"One date." I held up one finger. "I mean it, Jay. One date to prove that we can do this."

He raised one eyebrow. "Really?"

"Yes, really. But that's it—until it happens, nothing changes. If we're going to do this, we're going to do this properly."

His eyes glinted as he moved toward me. "As it happens, I have an idea."

"That scares me."

"I know." He pushed my bangs out of my eyes. "We changed how we live together because of *The Big Bang Theory*, so why don't we try another thing from the show to see if we can make our relationship work?"

It was my turn to raise my eyebrows. "I'm not writing a relationship agreement."

"Not that." He barely hid his laughter. "When Penny and Leonard got back together."

I frowned. "You want to beta test our relationship?"

"No. We should do our first date as if we don't know each other."

My lips twitched.

"There are probably things you'd tell a date that I don't know, so it'd be fun."

I tried not to laugh, but I couldn't help it. It was the craziest thing I'd ever heard, but somehow... it made sense.

"All right. I'll play. You tell me where and when, and I'll be there." I grabbed the dishcloth and tossed it at him. "I have to work. Be a dear and finish the dishes, would you?"

"Wow. Is this what I have to look forward to?"

I turned, walking backward. "Yes. You do live here after all."

His lips curved to one side in a smirk that made me want to kiss it. "Goddamn it, I do."

CHAPTER 19

Chore Charts Aren't Just For Kids

Jay

I'd fucking nailed it.

I had the best, most ridiculous, insane idea for our first date, and I was proud as fuck of it.

Now, I just had to get Shelby on board.

Granted, picking her parents' bar was a problem, but it was Friday night and it'd be busy because of their promotions. Her dad knew what was up, and I hoped he'd tell her mom because Lucy Daniels was a wildcard.

It was where Shelby got it from.

I stepped out of the elevator and paused. The unmistakable sound of the Backstreet Boys was blaring from our apartment, and I stopped for a second to stare at the door.

Had I gone back in time fifteen years?

What was going on inside there?

Tentatively, I made my way toward the door and pulled

my keys out. I unlocked the door and pushed it open, only to be greeted by one hell of a sight.

Shelby.

Mopping.

And singing.

Her hair was pulled on top of her head in a messy bun with tendrils escaping at the nape of her neck, curling against her skin. She wore a tight white tank top and hot-pink shorts that only just covered her ass.

That was swaying.

She was dancing. And she was singing. *Holy fuck*, was she singing. The mop was her own personal microphone, and she swung it to the right, her eyes closed, as she sang along to "I Want It That Way."

I was frozen to the spot. Mostly because it hit me that this was the kind of shit she did when she was alone. She'd spent the morning taking the piss out of me for singing Ed Sheeran in the shower, and here she was, singing Back-street Boys while mopping the floor.

This was the best thing I'd ever seen.

I pulled my phone from my pocket and set the camera to record. She had no idea I was here because she was blasting the music so loudly.

Oh, my fuck. She was performing a concert. This was the best thing I'd ever seen.

Screw her showing my baby pictures at my wedding.

This video was going online on her thirtieth birthday.

Or her wedding—whichever happened first. Not that I'd let her marry anyone but me, but whatever. That was moot right now.

Because the song was now fucking "MMMbop."

She continued on singing like she didn't have an audience. I guess in her mind, she didn't.

I loved that she apparently listened to nineties boyband pop while she cleaned alone.

I pushed the door open, stopped the video, and quietly walked over to her. The second the chorus kicked in, I grabbed her hips and pulled her against me, humming into her ear.

Shelby screamed, jumping away from me. She brandished the mop as a weapon while I laughed my fucking ass off.

"Oh, my God!" She shoved the mop at me, going to hit me with it. "You gave me a heart attack!"

"Turn the elementary school disco down then!"

She grabbed her phone from the island and turned the music down. "There." She scowled. "Better?"

"Yeah." I grinned. "Is this how you clean when I'm not here?"

Her cheeks blazed. "No comment."

Hell, I wanted to scoot forward and kiss her. "I want to tease you, but I won't. We're on borrowed time."

"We are?" She gripped the mop with both hands. "Why? Has Planet Earth been invaded by aliens with three penises?"

"What the hell are you ghostwriting?"

"You don't want to know." She shook her head. "Well? Has it?"

"Not to my knowledge." I dumped my bag by the door.

"But tonight is our first date."

Shelby's eyebrows shot up. "It is?"

"Uh-huh."

"You move fast."

"You have no idea." I wiggled my brows for emphasis.

Her cheeks flushed a fresh shade of pink. "All right, where are we going?"

"Your parents' bar."

"What?" The mop clattered to the floor. "Have you lost your ever-lovin' mind? Who wants their first date with their best friend in front of their parents?"

I held up my hands and darted behind the island to put some distance between us. "I told your dad. He's breaking it to your mom, but I think she already knew I liked you."

Shelby grunted, glaring at me.

"It's Friday night. I don't have to work tomorrow. It'll be busy. I have it planned out. C'mon." I gave her my best effort at puppy dog eyes.

It backfired.

She laughed instead of giving in. "There are hungry wolves who could look more innocent than that!"

"Come on. It'll be fun. I swear."

"You're paying all night," she warned me, since her parents didn't usually charge us when we were all together.

"Your dad already knows. He's opened a tab and whatever you want is on me."

She studied me for a second. "I'm not okay with this."

"You will be by the time we're done." My lips tugged

to one side. "I promise. You'll laugh your ass off the entire time."

"I don't think I trust you, Jay Cooper."

"You don't have to trust me. You just have to pretend you do." My tiny smile became a full-fledged grin, and though she fought her own smile, she eventually broke.

"Screw you!" She laughed, bending over to pick up the mop. "If my parents say anything—"

"They won't." I figured I was safe to come out from behind the island and approached her. She looked beautiful without her makeup, and I cupped her chin with my right hand. "Your parents' bar, eight-fifteen. Got it?"

She thrust the mop at me. "Got it. Finish this, would you? I have a hot date to get ready for."

She turned on her heel, stalking off toward the bathroom, and I laughed as I watched her go.

Maybe this wouldn't be the disaster I was afraid it would be.

Because let's be honest—it wasn't my best idea. Taking her to her parents' bar could go one of two ways, and if I hadn't caught her dad earlier and told him I was taking her out—much to his delight—I wouldn't be daring this so soon.

Fact was, I wanted her.

I wanted this date to happen as soon as possible. I wanted her as soon as possible—I wanted to redefine the parameters of our relationship, to go further than stupid make-out sessions.

I wanted more.

I wanted her. I wanted to *be* hers, even if she had yelled

at me before I left because I'd left a pan soaking in the sink and it'd turned the water grimy and I hadn't emptied it out.

It was worth it.

Fuck, it had to be worth it.

Shelby was already sitting at the bar when I got there. She was talking to her dad with her back to me, so I slid onto a stool at the empty table Tom had reserved for us. He caught my eye, and I couldn't believe I was pulling this off.

All right, so I was a little ahead of myself here. I'd only walked in and sat down. I still had to pull off the whole 'strangers' thing I'd suggested, something that seemed cuter on paper than in real life.

How did you explain yourself to the person who knew everything about you?

One of the servers brought a beer over to my table and I thanked him, just watching Shelby. She'd hidden in her room before I'd left, and now I saw why.

I'd never actually seen her on a date before. I usually saw her in yesterday's sweatpants and a tank top with crumbs all over it. That was her uniform, so seeing her like this was different.

Her dark hair fell over her shoulders, perfectly straight, and her body was hugged by a black dress that had a slit at her knee.

I almost didn't want to see her from the front. I didn't think I could take it if she looked this good from the back.

I nodded to her dad when he caught my eye again.

He leaned over the bar, pointing in my direction. Shelby turned her head, frowning at me.

I grinned.

She turned back to her dad for a brief second, then grabbed her wine glass and walked over to join me at the table.

I was right. I couldn't cope with how beautiful she looked. Her dress had a high neckline that left her arms totally bare, and she wore black high heels that made my eyebrows raise when I stood to greet her.

Touching her hip, I leaned over and kissed her cheek. "Hi. I'm Jay."

"Oh, my God." She laughed. "Are we really doing the stranger thing?"

"Yes." My lips twitched. "Hey—you're wearing high heels. Anything is possible."

She stuck her tongue in her cheek before she smiled and rolled her eyes. "You're ridiculous, you know that?"

"It's part of my charm."

"Did you have my dad keep me busy at the bar just to do this?"

I shook my head with a serious look on my face and pulled out her chair. "No. As a complete stranger, I've never met the man at the bar before."

Shelby covered her pink lips with her hand as she sat down. "This is the weirdest thing I've ever done, and I'm writing a book about aliens with three penises for a client."

"Oh, you're a writer?"

She looked like she didn't know whether to laugh or cry. It took her a minute before she sagged, smiling, even though it was clearly against her will. "All right. I'll play along. Even though this is totally stupid."

The grin on my face was so wide it was going to split my cheeks. "Let's start again. Hi. I'm Jay."

She took a deep breath, and the expression that flashed across her face told me she couldn't believe she was doing this. "I'm Shelby. It's nice to *meet* you, Jay."

She was right. This was ridiculous. But shit, we'd started it now, so we were going to see it through.

This was the last time I planned a first date.

"So, Shelby, what do you do for a living?"

Her lips twitched and she cradled her wine glass. "I'm a writer."

"Oh? What do you write?"

"Personally, I write romance, but I also do freelance research articles for local papers and ghostwrite."

"What's ghostwriting?" I leaned forward. And, hey, it was a valid question. I wasn't actually entirely sure.

"Other people hire me to write books for them. Depending on how much work they want done, some people will send me a rough outline and I'll start from scratch, but others will send me a really rough draft and have me rework it into a proper book."

"Sounds interesting. What do you usually write for that?"

"Anything. I've written romance, paranormal, fantasy... Right now, I'm ghostwriting a book about aliens invading Earth."

"Fun."

Her eyes glittered. "They have three penises."

My lips twitched. "And you're officially the most interesting first date I've ever had."

She laughed, flicking her hair over her shoulder. "What do you do?"

"My dad owns a chain of gyms across Texas, and I manage the one here in town."

She flicked her gaze to my arms, then leaned forward on the table and rested her chin on her fingers. "Oh? So you work out?"

She was deliberately being overly-flirtatious in an attempt to get me to stop this stupid charade, but it was so much fun, I couldn't.

Now, I wanted to keep it up to see which one of us would break first.

"Now and then," I said, smirking. "What do you do for fun? Do you have any interesting hobbies?"

"Not really. I work a lot, so I mostly spend my free time watching TV and telling my roommate to pick up his dirty socks and food wrappers."

Great. That's how this was going to go. Point: Shelby.

"You have a roommate?"

"Mm." Her lips pulled into the tiniest smile. "We've been friends for years, but he's a bit of a dork. Only just figured out how to use a washing machine. The dishwasher is still a little foreign to him, but he remembered to clean the sink out after he shaved today, so I figure I'm making progress in training him to be the perfect roommate."

It was so fucking hard not to laugh. Training me my ass.

The worst part? It was all true, and that's why it was so damn funny. She'd gone into the bathroom after I'd shaved, and two minutes later, she'd found me in the living room with a bright yellow Post-It note.

She'd drawn a smiley face on it and wrote, "I cleaned up after myself!"

Then she'd stuck it onto my t-shirt before running away.

I sincerely hoped that wasn't going to be a new tradition.

"Nobody's perfect," I replied. "In fact, I have a roommate, too."

"Oh?" She raised one eyebrow, sipping her wine.

"Yeah. Like your roommate, we've been friends for years. She's a little bit neurotic at times, especially if you eat her Oreos, but she makes some mean pancakes. I don't even care that she yells at me about all my shortcomings, because yesterday I found a Kit-Kat wrapper stashed in the bathroom drawer and I know it isn't mine."

Shelby pursed her lips and looked away for a second. "Maybe she likes to snack in the bath."

"She also likes to sing while she mops and uses the mop as a microphone. She's a little bit crazy."

"Sometimes a little bit of crazy is a good thing."

Slowly, I curved my lips into a smile. "A little bit of crazy is definitely a good thing."

CHAPTER 20

No Judging On Snacking Habits

Shelby

A little bit of crazy was a good thing, but this date was a lot of crazy.

Yet, at the same time, it was kinda cute. It was fun to talk to each other and tease him the way I just had, and I wasn't going to lie and say my stomach wasn't fluttering like hell.

It was.

I was nervous.

I hadn't expected to be. After all, I knew Jay. But this set-up, pretending like we were strangers, was weird. It actually felt like a real first date, no matter how stupid it was and how ridiculous I felt.

Mostly, I was nervous because I didn't go home with someone after a first date.

Tonight, I didn't have a choice. What would happen

when we got there? Would we just disappear into our own rooms? Would there be another sexually frustrating make-out session on the couch?

Would there be a make-out session that led to more?

I didn't usually sleep with someone on the first date, but as I said: I didn't have to go home with them after.

For now, though, I wanted to carry on pretending we didn't know each other. I'd never wanted to laugh as much as I had in the last fifteen minutes, and since laughter was a measuring stick of mine for dating anyway, he was doing pretty good.

Even if he was a dork for this idea.

"Tell me about your family," Jay said, leaning forward a little more. His eyes flashed with laughter, like he knew just how stupid it was.

"Well, my parents own this bar."

"Shit. This is awkward, isn't it?"

Oh, my God. Stop it.

"Just a little bit."

"Who are your parents?"

This is so ridiculous.

"My dad is the tall guy with not a lot of hair, and my mom is the one with dark, curly hair."

"Ah. I see where you get your good looks from."

I bit my lip to stop myself laughing. "Don't say that to her. She might start planning our wedding."

Jay gave me an over-exaggerated wink. It was something he'd said to her every single time he wanted something, and it always ended up with Mom whipping him

211

with whichever cloth she had in her hand at the time.

"What about your family?" I asked, hiding my grin by drinking from my wine.

"My dad owns a small chain of gyms as I said, and my mom mostly does the books for them. She's an accountant by trade."

"So it's a family thing."

"Pretty much." He smiled. "Then there's my grand-mother. She's terrified of snakes but has a tiny dog who likes to bring them to her as presents, and she's developed a habit of guilting me into going to see her and doing things for her."

"I'm not a fan of snakes, either, to be honest. Spiders I can do, but not snakes."

"Really? Even the big spiders?" His eyebrows shot up, even though his eyes were shining with mirth.

"Yep. They don't bother me. But snakes?" I shuddered. "They're slimy and remind me too much of worms."

"Fair comparison." He lifted his beer and closed his lips around the rim of it to take a drink.

I took that second to look around. The bar was busy, and the line of sight between us and my parents had disap-peared thanks to all the people who'd filtered in since we'd been here. The volume of the music had slowly crept up over the last half an hour, and some of the tables that were usually reserved for food had been moved to clear an area for dancing.

There was already a throng of people there. Men and women, dancing in twosomes and in groups, and a few were crowded around the modern-style jukebox Mom had installed only a few weeks ago. It was fun because of how it linked up to the main stereo; it waited until the programmed song was done before it started a new one.

It also meant that the music on Thursdays, Fridays, and Saturdays was almost exclusively chosen by the customers. Which meant that one minute you were dancing to the latest song from say, Calvin Harris, and the next thing you knew, you were rocking out to Elvis.

It was hilarious.

Jay followed my gaze. "You wanna dance?"

As a rule, no, but this was a date. "Sure. Why not?"

His eyebrows shot up in surprise, but he followed my lead in finishing off his drink. We stood, and he took my hand, pulling me through the people and toward the dance-floor in front of the jukebox.

Grinning, he pulled me into the middle of the crowd and toward his body. His hands trailed to my hips, and he waggled his eyebrows as the song became more upbeat. He made me sway my hips side to side, and I laughed, gripping onto his arms and he exaggerated every movement.

It was so, so fun.

We danced for a few songs, our bodies moving together, until he put one finger to his lips and slinked off toward the jukebox. I frowned, basically standing still until he came back with a grin on his face.

"What did you choose?" I asked into his ear.

"It's a secret!" he said back as "The Birdie Song" came on.

"If this was you—"

He burst out laughing, quickly pulling me into him.

"No. Mine's next."

I tried to escape the mess that was the dance routine to this song, but Jay wasn't having it. He tugged me back, linking his arm through mine, and spun us around. I squealed as my shoes pinched my toes, but I could barely breathe through my laughter.

Have you ever seen a six-foot-something, muscular, book-cover-model-worthy man do the freaking birdie dance?

It was possibly the best thing I'd ever seen. He got so into it, shaking his ass and waggling his eyebrows as he did the hand movements. I bent over laughing, holding my stomach. I laughed so hard I had to grab hold of him before I fell over, and he responded by winding his arm around my waist and pulling me against him.

His firm body was shaking with laughter, and he pressed his cheek against the side of my head as the song died.

Only to be replaced with the one song I should have known he'd put on.

Ed. Freakin'. Sheeran.

"Noooo," I groaned, flattening my hands against his chest.

"My roommate loves it when I sing this in the shower," he said into my ear, his laughter barely restrained. "I could give Ed a run for his money."

"I have no idea how to respond to that," I replied right as he started singing in my ear, making my body move with his.

No matter how I tried to pull away, he gripped me tighter, singing deliberately more awful than usual. It was horrendous, honestly. To have the beautiful tones of Ed Sheeran in one ear and the cat-strangling voice of Jay Cooper in the other.

I leaned my head back and met his eyes. He was only mouthing the song now, but he was such an idiot, making the funniest expressions as he did it, and I had to laugh. My stomach hurt from laughing so much in the last few minutes.

His eyes sparkled, even in the dim light. They were so bright, and he was looking at me with such happiness that I really wasn't responsible for the fact I leaned up and kissed him.

It just happened.

Really.

I pulled back and blushed.

Slowly, he smiled. He slid one of his hands up to the back of my neck and lowered his face to mine, his lips brushing over mine several times until the song changed to something more upbeat and he grabbed my hand and spun me on the spot.

I fell against him, unprepared, and through my own laughter, I could hear the deep rumble of his in his chest.

Maybe this really was worth the risk.

Jay handed the cab driver fifteen dollars and helped me out of the car. We were still breathless from dancing and laughing for the better part of two hours, and even though we didn't live far from the bar, there was no way I could walk.

My feet were screaming at me. I didn't wear heels, ever, so I could barely walk. I only just made it inside the building before I used the wall to prop myself up so I could take the damn things off.

I moaned as they came off and my toes finally had some freedom.

Jay laughed, hitting the button for the elevator. "Do you think that cab driver thought we were having a one-night stand?"

I shrugged, grinning. "Think of it this way—there'd be no walk of shame."

"I don't know, that ten feet between our bedroom doors is one helluva stroll."

I hobbled into the elevator after him. "Yeah, and that window at the end of the hall could really give things away."

He looped one arm around my waist. "Are your feet okay?"

"No."

He did a double-take before a laugh snorted out of him. "I told you we should have sat out the Cha Cha Slide."

"Are you kidding me? After seeing you do the Birdie dance, I had to see you do that. I was kinda sad nobody put the Macarena on."

The doors opened, and he helped me out. "Yeah, especially after the line-dancing club came in in their cowgirl finery."

"Oh, my God. Don't. I'll never look at seventy-some-thing-year-old women in denim skirts and cowboy boots the same again." I shook my head as he fished his keys out of his pocket.

Apparently, it was the fifteen-year anniversary of the club being formed, and so they'd thrown it back to their younger days with their outfits. Let's just say their skirts were a little on the short side.

"I think your dad is scarred for life." Jay pushed the door open.

"Well, he's not much of a dancer. Especially when he's being shared by ten women who could be his mother." I dropped my heels next to the shoe stand and pushed the door shut. "If they ever come in again, he's going to hide out the back."

"Especially since the leader of the club gave him her number."

"It was after their third round of tequila shots."

Yeah. It'd been that kind of night, and we only had one drink each.

We'd been too amused to even think about getting another.

I took the bottle of water he handed me and looked up at him through my lashes. "I had fun tonight."

His grin was lopsided. "So did I. Even if the whole beginning of it was the stupidest thing ever."

"I said it was!" I laughed for the hundredth time tonight. "But you demanded we carry it on."

"Yeah, but wouldn't it have been awkward otherwise?"

"Maybe." I fiddled with the label on the bottle. "Do you really think it helped?"

"What else would we have talked about? Our mutual friends?" Jay snorted and walked over to me, bopping me on the nose so I scowled. "It is weird. We both know that. In a strange way, it took away all that weirdness despite how fucking ridiculous it was."

He was right. It really did take it all away. "All right. I admit it wasn't a bad idea. But you are a terrible dancer."

"I'm an excellent dancer, I'll have you know. I rocked the shit out of that tweet-tweet song."

"Five-year-olds can do those moves."

"Yeah, but their arms don't look as good as mine." He wiggled his eyebrows. "That's the selling point for me."

"That was also why you looked absolutely ridiculous doing it."

"Ha!" He tapped my nose again. "I knew you were perving on me."

"Well, yeah. Have you seen your ass?" I clapped my hand over my mouth.

I was not supposed to say that out loud.

"I have, and it's a pretty great one. Why do you think I sing that Ed Sheeran song in the shower? I'm admiring the shape of *me*. I can see it in the mirror until the door steams up."

I blinked at him, then turned around and rolled my eyes. And he said I was the crazy one.

His laughter followed me as he did, and I turned at my bedroom door. "Goodnight, Jay."

"Hang on." He undid the top button of his shirt and took my bottle of water to set on the floor. His eyes found mine, and he gave me a sexy half-smile that made my heart stutter. "If we didn't live together, I'd have kissed you at the door, but since I don't want to sleep in the hall…"

I raised an eyebrow. "Really? Why not? I bet the whirring of the elevator is very soothing."

He pressed one finger against my lips despite his chuckle and pulled me to him. His eyes searched mine for the longest moment, and I took a deep breath, resting my hands on his chest.

I smiled.

So did he.

Jay dipped his head and kissed me slowly. I savored every second. The more he kissed me, the easier it was to forget who we were to each other.

Right now, as he moved his lips over mine and made my heart beat faster and faster, he wasn't my best friend. I could almost imagine that he was nobody more than a guy I'd met who I liked. Who I'd been on a date with. Who I didn't want to leave at the door.

Could I?

Could I pull him into my room and have sex with him? At this point, there was really no turning back anyway.

It was a little painful to admit, but Jay was everything I'd ever wanted in a guy. He could be sweet, he made me laugh more than anyone else, his smile gave me butterflies, he could turn me on with one tiny kiss...

I could see it. I could see a relationship working.

I mean, he did clean the sink after he'd shaved earlier, and that was pretty sexy.

I gripped his shirt tightly and pulled him backward toward my bedroom door.

"Shelby?" he said against my mouth.

"Yeah?"

"Have you thought this through?"

"Yes. I figure we've already reached the point of no return." I leaned against my closed door, hand on the handle, and gazed up at him. "You saw me singing into a mop and still want to date me, so we may as well go the whole way before I get the giggles again."

He smirked. "True. That was quite the hit to my ego."

"Then shut up and come here before it happens again." I dragged him to me as I opened the door.

He captured my hips with his hands as he kissed me. The heat that had teased me only minutes earlier rushed through me with a vengeance. It was fire when we touched, and in mere seconds, my body came completely alive.

My fingers were already fumbling with the buttons on his shirt. I was more excited than I should have been for this moment. I'd had his abs paraded around in front of me for weeks, and now they were finally mine to touch.

It was like Christmas but for my clitoris.

I finally got the last button undone as he reached up for the zipper for my dress. I slipped my hands inside his shirt, pressing them against his sides, and he hissed in a breath.

"How the hell are your hands so cold?"

"They match my heart," I quipped.

"Says the romance writer."

"Keep talking; I'll start a murder mystery, and you'll be my first victim."

He chuckled, unzipping my dress in one swift movement. "No, I won't." He lowered his lips back to mine before I could retort, and I melted against his body.

Man, he really could kiss.

The gentle ache between my legs became a more urgent throb of need, and I whimpered as he took my lower lip between his teeth. It was like there was a direct jolt of pleasure straight between my legs, and he smiled against my lips, gripping my ass.

It pressed my body flush against his. His cock was rock solid, pressing against my stomach, and my hips rocked involuntarily.

His tongue stroked the seam of my mouth, and I met his with mine, deepening the kiss. Each kiss tugged at something deep inside me, and by the time he slid his hands up to pull my dress down, I was about ready to plead for him to get on with it.

Goosebumps coated my skin as he pushed my dress down. It pooled at my feet and I stepped out of it.. I shrank three inches as I did so, and Jay jolted, laughing as the kiss broke because of our height difference.

He shucked off his shirt and guided me to the bed. I barely had a chance to be conscious of my body before he covered it with his and kissed me again.

I wanted to wrap myself around him and not let go. It was becoming a recurring feeling whenever he kissed me, but it was particularly strong now that his skin was directly against mine.

He was too clothed right now, but I was about to rectify that.

I reached between us and tugged on the belt loops on his jeans. He got the hint, sitting up. I propped myself up on my hands and watched as he undid the button and the zipper, never taking his eyes off me.

He didn't say a word as he dropped them to the floor

and stepped out of them.

He even stopped to take off his socks.

Now *that* was sexy.

"Make sure you pick those up," I muttered when he resumed position over me, and I was on my back again.

He laughed, grazing his teeth over my lower lip. "I love how you're practically naked under me and all you can think about is the roommate agreement."

"It's not all I can think about," I argued. "Besides, the rules are there for a reason."

"Yeah?" He dropped his head and kissed along my jaw. "What about the rules about pants and wearing proper clothes?"

I gasped as he pulled my hips snug against his and his cock pressed against my sensitive clitoris. "Those rules are temporarily suspended."

"That's what I thought." He kissed me again, pulling my legs up so they were hooked over his hips. I ran my fingers up his arms and over his shoulders, down his chest and stomach and back up his sides, exploring every inch of him I could reach while he rocked his hips against mine.

I moaned. At this rate, he wouldn't even need to be inside me. I'd come from the pressure of him against me alone. I was wet as hell, and when another tiny moan escaped me, Jay smiled against my mouth.

He adjusted his body just enough so that he could reach down between us. His fingers trailed across my stomach until they slipped beneath my panties, moving through my wetness. His thumb brushed my clit, and I shuddered, cupping the back of his neck to keep his mouth on mine.

He teased me, fully moving my panties to the side, and ran two fingers over my clit and down farther. He eased them inside me, one at a time, and my hips moved to give him easier access.

I gasped into his mouth as he moved his hand, fucking me with his fingers while he did the same to my mouth with his tongue. Heat prickled across my skin, especially when his thumb touched my clit.

My hips bucked into his hand, and I moaned, pressing myself against him.

But he didn't let me come.

Nope.

Slowly, he withdrew his fingers from me when I was on the very brink of orgasm, and my next moan was for a whole damn different reason.

"Not fair," I murmured when he moved and gripped the waistband of his boxers.

He grinned shamelessly, letting go of his underwear and taking hold of mine instead. He pulled them swiftly down my legs and tossed them onto the floor before he turned his attention back to his own.

Jay stood and was just about to take his boxers down when he paused. "Do you have a condom?"

I opened my mouth, then froze.

I did *not*.

"Do *you* have a condom?" I shot back.

He shook his head.

"What the hell? Not even in your wallet? Aren't guys supposed to carry them everywhere? Is that all a myth? I feel so betrayed."

He fought his laughter. "Well, I haven't had sex in nine months, so why would I have some? I thought you would since you dragged me in here."

"I don't!" I pulled the pillow from just above my head and smothered myself with it, screaming into it.

He didn't even try to hide his laugh this time. The pillow was yanked out of my hands, and he leaned over me. "Shelby. I know you're on the pill. Do you trust me?"

I met his stunning green gaze. I knew what he was asking. He wanted to do this without a condom.

"More than anyone else," I replied, leaning up to kiss him.

He returned it enthusiastically, pausing only to finally take off his damn underwear. I reached between us and wrapped my hand around his shaft, slowly pumping my fist. He was long and thick, the perfect size, and the more I touched him, the more turned on I was.

His kisses got deeper as he got harder, and when he fisted hair at the nape of my neck and tugged my head back so he could kiss down to my collarbone, I adjusted my hips, rubbing the head of his cock against my clit.

It felt so damn good that I just wanted to keep doing that until I came, but I wanted him more, so I slipped him inside me, slowly taking him deeper and deeper.

He groaned into my mouth, one hand down at my ass and gripping it tightly. He rocked into me, taking it slow and easy. I ran my hands over his body again and wrapped my legs around his waist, kissing him as he moved.

I felt him everywhere. Jay being inside me was like a drug—I didn't know if I would be able to get enough of this sensation. I was hooked, gripping onto his shoulders as he moved faster, pumping his cock inside me as if he was forcing my orgasm out from me.

He didn't have to force hard. It was building, swirling through my veins in a kaleidoscope of sensations. Hair stood up on my arms. Goosebumps prickled across my breasts. Muscles twitched in my legs. And it was pure pleasure, taking me on a high, hurtling through my body as I tightened my grip on him wherever I was touching him.

He joined me right as I was coming down from the high, groaning my name into the side of my neck. His lips burned where he touched me, and as I ran my fingers through his hair, still breathing heavily, I knew one thing.

Everything had changed.

CHAPTER 21

No Pants Are The Best Pants

Shelby

"**W**e need to talk."

Jay blinked at me. "I just stepped through the door."

"Really? I thought you'd flown in through the window." I rolled my eyes. "In light of the changing circumstances in our relationship, we need to talk."

"Oh, good," he drawled, shutting the door behind him and dumping his gym bag. "Those are the four words anyone likes to hear less than twenty-four hours after sex."

I shot him a withering look. "I ordered food."

"Is it pizza?"

"I got salad with it."

"Your diet—"

"Is shit, I know, and I don't care right now." I grinned and pointed my pen at him. "We need to discuss the roommate agreement."

He eyed me speculatively as he pulled juice from the fridge. "You're not going to make me sign a relationship agreement, are you?"

"No. We're not quite there yet."

"Shelby, we had one date, and where did I wake up this morning?" He quirked a brow. "In your bed. I think we're there."

"We had one date. Unless we have another and agree to be exclusive, we're not there."

"All right. Let's go out tonight, and you're now my girlfriend. How does that sound?"

He was insufferable. "You can't just declare that I'm your girlfriend. Relationships aren't dictatorships. You can't make that decision."

"Fine. Then I'm your boyfriend. Either way, we're now exclusive." He smirked and leaned forward on the island, making his biceps strain against his t-shirt.

"That's really not fair when you do that."

"Are you wearing a bra right now?"

I swallowed and looked down. Hi, nipples. "I've been working all day. Frankly, you're lucky I'm wearing pants."

"I'd like to argue and call that unlucky."

Any day where pants were required was an unlucky one in my opinion. Then again, I had spent the whole day wearing just panties, fluffy socks, and a tank top, so maybe today wasn't all *that* bad.

"Which brings me to my first point of discussion. Rule one: must wear pants." I tapped the pen against it. "I propose that all points regarding wearing clothing be removed."

Jay leaned forward, his lips twisting upward. "I'm listening."

"I discovered last night that, actually, I'm quite fond of no pants, so rule one should be: no pants are the best pants."

"Done."

I pursed my lips. "How did I know there would be absolutely no resistance from you with that one?"

He held his hands up before grabbing his water. "I am extremely fond of you with no pants. In fact, feel free to remove yours right now if you'd be more comfortable."

I rested my elbows on the island and pointed my pen at him again. "You didn't pick up your socks this morning. The only way you're getting inside these pants is if you take them off."

"Is that an offer?"

"Not until you pick up your freakin' socks."

"What is it with you and socks? They're right up there with Oreos. Borderline obsession."

I shrugged. "I'm a tidy person with unhealthy eating habits. What can I say?"

"One day, you'll come to the gym with me." He wiggled the bottle at me.

"Absolutely not." I shook my head. "You know those couples where you look at them and you're like, 'Whoa, shit, he's punching?' That's what's going to happen here. I'll sit with my extra fifteen pounds snuggling my ass, thighs, and boobs, and you can sit there miserable because you have to work out to look that good."

"You have an extra fifteen pounds? Where?"

I opened my mouth, stopping when I saw his smirk. "More responses like that, and I'll take my pants off by-myself."

"Good. If you have an extra five pounds on your ass— and I think you're full of shit—I happen to be a fan of that."

"You're pushing it now."

He shrugged. "I don't care. You see an extra fifteen pounds; I see hot as fuck. It works."

My cheeks flushed. "Yes, well…"

"You really are adorable when you're embarrassed."

I hit him with a look, pursing my lips so I didn't smile at him. "Next up: we have to assume that at some point, if I don't kill you, you'll move into my room."

"Wait. Why am I moving into your room?" He flattened his hands on the island.

"Would you like to sleep in your room tonight know-ing that me and my extra fifteen pounds of hotness are on the other side of the wall? In the bigger bedroom?"

He went to say something then stopped, shaking his head. "That would last all of about ten minutes. I can't sleep with my hand cupping your boob if there's a wall between us."

Yeah. That was way more comfortable for him than me. It didn't matter that it was comfortable when *I* put my hand on my boob. I bet it wouldn't be comfortable for him if I spent the entire night with my hand on his cock.

"You know, for someone who said we weren't exclu-sive, sharing a room is pretty damn serious." Laughter glinted in his eyes.

I shrugged. "I'm a planner. I like to plan. Like I said, it all depends on whether I kill you or not. We might not even make it past three dates."

"We'll make it past three dates."

"How are you so sure?"

"Because." He walked around the island, coming to me, and spun me around on the stool. He plucked the pen from my fingers and set it down, smiling down at me.

"Because what?"

His fingers tingled as they brushed my skin and pushed some hair behind my ear. "Because three dates means you're my girlfriend whether you like it or not, and then nobody else ever has to see my embarrassing baby pictures."

My lips thinned. "It's nice to know you want to date me to keep those under wraps."

"I figure you'll find a way to share them with just about everyone at some point," he continued. "But this will delay it for a couple of years, at least."

"I think you're insane. I might put them on Facebook tomorrow. Your mom will share them with me in a heartbeat."

"My mother is a traitor."

"She's the best. I might date you just so I can eventually marry you and have her be my mother-in-law."

"So you'd marry me for my mother?"

I nodded. "You go find yourself another girl like that. Go on. I'll wait."

He trapped me against the island by putting his hands on either side of me. "I don't want to find another girl like that. I like the one I have in front of me just fine."

"I've gone from hot as fuck to just fine really fast."

"Yeah, but you've gone from liking me without pants on to marrying me for my mother, so we're about even."

I grinned, leaning back on my elbows. "Well I'm not ever going to marry you for your domestic skills, that's for sure."

"Ah, but that's why I'd marry you. I'm good in bed; you're good with a vacuum…"

"I could knee you in the balls right now, and then the only thing you'd be in bed would be useless."

He laughed, leaning closer to me. "Ah, are we out of the honeymoon phase already?"

"Jay, the honeymoon phase upped and left the day you moved in here. It'll start again when you pick up your socks."

"Fucking socks." He pushed off the island and stormed toward the hall.

The sound of my bedroom door opening and closing filled the air, and I laughed when he came back in, waved the socks, and stalked off to his room to toss them in the laundry basket.

"I picked up the damn socks," he announced, coming back over to stand in front of me. "Are you happy now?"

"Would you like another Post-It sticker? I have tons."

"No, I don't want a fucking sticker. Honestly, woman, do you hear yourself?"

"Yes. I think I'm a genius." I shrugged and looked up at

him. "I wish someone would give me stickers. Like, 'hey, Shelby, you hit your word count today! Have a sticker.' Or, I answered all my emails. Or I cleared my to-do list. A girl needs some motivation, you know."

"If I promise to buy you stickers tomorrow, will you take your pants off?" He raised his eyebrows in question.

"Depends how good the stickers are." I wiggled my eyebrows as there was a knock at the door. That would be dinner.

I grabbed my wallet from the island and paid the guy, then took the pizza box and the salad containers and kicked the door shut behind him.

"Only one pizza?" Jay raised his eyebrows. "You surprise me."

"Not really. It's only pepperoni. I'm not putting any vegetables on my pizza." I put everything down on the island and sat back down on the stool, putting the roommate agreement aside.

"Do we still need that now?" Jay sat next to me and pointed to the agreement. "I mean, I think we have it pretty figured out. I'm not the slob I once was."

"It's been two weeks since we put it together. You've done your laundry three times, and don't think I didn't notice you slipping t-shirts into my basket."

"Shit. You noticed?"

"Yes. Funnily enough, I'm not a men's large. I noticed."

He gave me his sexiest smile. "I bet you'd look good in one, though."

"Stop trying to charm me." I wiggled my finger at him

and prodded him in the shoulder. "We're not in a relationship yet. We're going to figure this out slowly. It doesn't matter if we had sex last night—if having sex once is the criteria for being in a relationship, there are a whole lot of people out there cheating on their partners."

He chuckled, leaning over to get cutlery for the salads from the drawer next to the fridge. "You've never had a one-night stand, have you?"

"No. Because according to you, that equals a relationship."

"You're twisting my words." He rolled his eyes. "We're not in a relationship because we had sex. If anything, we're in one for the same reason most people are. Because they have feelings for each other."

"I have a lot of feelings for you. Some romantic. Some good. Some bad." I opened the pizza box and peered at him out of the side of my eyes. "I can keep you on your toes that way."

"Okay, okay, fine. I understand. We're not in a relationship. Don't come crying to me when you want to be in one." He shrugged one shoulder, but his lips were twitching. "I'll be emotionally unavailable."

I stared at him. "Really? And you think I'm the crazy one?"

"I'm playing hard to get."

"You're doing a terrible job." I looked pointedly at his pants where I could see his cock was hard.

"You're not wearing a bra!" He waved his hand at my chest. "If you don't want me to be turned on by you, wear a bra."

I picked up a slice of pizza. "When did I say I didn't

want you to be turned on by me?"

"Oh, so you won't be my girlfriend, but I can walk around with a hard cock and that's all right?"

"That's fine by me. It's useful if it's hard."

He stared at me for a long moment, then shook his head. "Of all the people I could have picked to have feelings for, it was you. Six billion people in the world, and I chose you."

I nudged him with my elbow, offering up my sweetest smile. "And I think that means you have excellent taste."

"You aren't wrong."

"You had sex once. Don't you need to figure out how to be in a relationship first?" Brie dipped her fry into ketchup.

We were back at my parents' bar for girls' night, except we were meeting both Sean and Jay after this. So, naturally, we were taking our sweet-ass time. Mostly because I needed her opinion on all this.

"Although," she went on. "You should have figured that out maybe before you had sex."

I rolled my eyes. "Listen—we'd already crossed the line. We'd both admitted how we felt. Going on a date with him was fun, Brie. It was the most fun I'd ever had with anyone, and it felt right."

"Then why not just be in a relationship? I know you're a bit of a relationship-phobe—"

"I am not a relationship-phobe!" I pulled my glass of Coke toward me. "I'm just...reserved with my emotions, but he already knows how I feel. It's not like we're getting into a normal relationship. We live together. We're going from zero to one-hundred, and we need to ease ourselves into that."

"Did you sleep in your bed last night?"

"Yes."

"Were you alone?"

I shoved a chicken tender in my mouth. "No comment," I said around a mouthful of food.

Brie smirked. "So you've had sex twice. You're at least at the fuck-buddy stage of being in a relationship. Fuck buddies with feelings. That's sticky."

"Yeah, and it's sticky before feelings," I muttered. "Regardless, I don't see why we need to label it. Why can't we just figure it out as it happens? Let it evolve naturally?"

"I think you've realized what you've done and now you're trying to backpedal," she said, putting down the half of her burger she'd been holding. She turned knowing eyes on me. "Your issue ever since you told me you had feelings for Jay was the fact he was your best friend. It was all centered around that. Not the fact that you had them—the fact you had them for *him*. You've talked about it already. You're the one who decided to make a go of it. Get your shit together."

I stared at her. I hated it when she was right. She was right now, and she knew that I knew it.

"If your friendship is that strong, breaking up is going to be awkward for a little bit, but you'll get through it. Hell, if you fight, he and I can swap places. I'll come live with you for a few days, and he can live with Sean. God knows I need a break every now and then. I keep suggesting saving up for the Bahamas, but he wants to come with me." She winked.

"I'll come instead. I think a vacation is what I need."

"The last time we went on vacation, you took a notebook to the beach."

"If inspiration can strike on the toilet, it can strike on the beach."

Brie rolled her eyes. "I know. You wrote half a book by hand."

I grinned.

"I'm just saying that everything can be changed. Hell, if you're really uncomfortable, tell him you've changed your mind."

"I haven't changed my mind. I just want us to move at as normal a pace as we can. Most people don't live together when they start a relationship."

"Okay, I get that. That makes more sense than you being freaked out about being in a relationship at all." She shoved two fries in her mouth and tilted her head as she chewed. "Although," she said when she'd swallowed them. "I feel like I should be surprised that you're dating each other, but I'm not. You just kinda...fit together. You're a lot more uptight than he is, but he's a hot damn mess for a grown-ass man. You make him a more responsible person, and he encourages you to have more fun. Somehow, you just work."

I sighed, trailing my chicken tender through the ketchup on my plate. "First, I resent you saying I'm uptight."

"You are uptight."

"That doesn't mean you have to say it." I sniffed.

"But you're right. We do balance each other out. I always thought that was why our friendship worked as well as it does, but maybe that's the perfect basis for a real relationship."

"Exactly. And think about it like this: you've already worked out the kinks in your relationship thanks to the roommate agreement. You both know what pisses the other person off. Like how Jay never wears pants."

"Oh." I held up my chicken. "We changed that yesterday. Instead of the rule being 'must wear pants,' it's now 'no pants are the best pants.'"

"And that's how you ended up having sex twice in two days."

"No. I ended up having sex twice in two days because sex with Jay is pretty damn great."

"And that's enough for me," Dad said, turning on his heel as soon as he arrived at the table.

My cheeks flamed. Brie laughed so hard she choked on her own spit. That was single-handedly the worst moment of my life. My dad knew we'd been on a date—obviously—but now he knew his daughter had sex on the first date.

Did that rule count since we lived together?

I know one date that wouldn't count—eating dinner at home. We did that, oh, every night?

I snorted to myself at the thought. Maybe I was taking the whole idea of dating Jay too literally. I was thinking about actually dating. Movies, restaurants, days out, nights out, drinks at a bar…

That wasn't really viable for us. Plus, we didn't need that time to get comfortable around each other. We already were. He'd seen me at my deadline worst with three-day-old sweatpants and hair that hadn't been washed for five days. I'd seen him with a little too much overgrown stubble and wing sauce on his shirt after a late night watching football.

Jesus, I was overthinking this.

This was the problem when you wrote books for a living. Mostly everything had to be thought through, and it wasn't always a good skill to bring into real life.

I blew out a long breath and looked at Brie, smiling. "I'm overreacting, aren't I?"

She grinned. "Do you need me to answer that?"

CHAPTER 22

Communication Is Key, Unless You Ate The Oreos

Jay

"**S**o what are you doing?" Sean asked, leaning against the side railing of the pier.

A gentle breeze whipped around me as I dropped my head back and looked at the darkening sky. "Figuring it all out. It ain't easy, you know? It's been four days—four fuckin' days since we admitted how we feel about each other."

"In other words, Shelby's phoning it in."

I looked at him out of the side of my eye. He wasn't exactly wrong, but it didn't bother me. I knew Shelby, and the fact that she'd even admitted to my face that she had feelings for me was something.

It was a fucking breakthrough, that was what it was.

"She's dealing with stuff in her own way," I replied. "It's not easy for her to talk about emotion. It never has been. I might tease her, but I'm never going to pressure her into doing something she isn't ready for. If she wants to casually date, fine. She wants to exclusively date, fine. It's all her prerogative. It doesn't mean she doesn't have feelings for me."

Sean grunted. "I dunno how you deal with it. Brie's so open about everything. It'd drive me crazy figuring out what's going on."

"Man, you need to remember they're different people. Brie is the extrovert to Shelby's introvert. Brie could spend all night in the middle of a club, dancing with strangers. That would give Shelby an anxiety attack. She'd rather lie in bed with a book."

"I get that. It's why they've been stuck to each other like glue since they were fuckin' eight." He snorted. "I guess I don't understand how you can trust how she feels."

"She told me."

"She told you the feeling was mutual."

"Exactly. Do you know how hard that was for her?" I turned and looked at him. "She was terrified to tell me that. We've been best friends for twenty years. Shelby isn't the kind of person to do anything on a whim."

"I know. She took me shopping for Brie's birthday. We went to two towns and thirteen stores."

I smirked. If that didn't sum Shelby up… "She's flaked on every serious relationship she's ever come close to having. Nobody has ever understood her. She's not afraid of commitment, she's just private. Ironic, really, considering she's happy to admit that she puts a piece of her soul into every single book she writes."

"We're different people. Not knowing exactly how she felt… Shit, Jay, even when Brie's mad at me, I know exactly how she feels." He gave me an exhausted look. "Her ass makes sure she details every single thing."

"You're talking about a woman who put a roommate agreement in front of me to tell me exactly how she felt. The first thing she did yesterday was outlaw wearing pants in the apartment. That tells me a lot."

It was also my new favorite rule, for what it was worth.

She'd worn a dress this morning.

If I hadn't had to go to work, we would have made it three-for-three on the sex timetable before lunch.

Sean laughed, shoving his hands in his pockets. "Well, if that ain't love…"

"You're a step ahead of us there." I joined him in laughing. "It's the little shit like that. She's hard work, but hell, I've put up with it for twenty years already."

"I thought you weren't in love with her."

"I'm not. That doesn't mean I don't love her, though. I do. I love her and have for years. It's complicated."

"Yeah, because now you live with her, and she's not just the cute friend you go to for advice."

I glanced at him. "She's the one I go to other people about."

"Exactly." He shrugged. "You make sense to me. Let's face it: you fuckin' suck at being an adult. Your grandma washed your clothes until recently. She's a good influence on you."

"She always has been." I looked out over the pier. At the food stalls, the lights, the tourist-centric rides, and arcades that brought people to our little coastal town.

What I was saying was true. The crazy, sweet, quiet,

sarcastic, kooky woman who was my best friend was a good influence on me.

We just really needed to figure out what we were to each other.

I think I already knew what she was to me. It felt so trivial to say that she was my kind of forever because if I was honest, I'd never imagined a future without Shelby in it.

Maybe that was my first clue.

Not once had I ever seen a future without her, but I'd never seen one with her on the sidelines, either.

She'd always been front and central, an integral part of my life.

Even if she avoided the gym like the plague. The same one I'd own one day.

I chuckled to myself. Jesus, we were the total opposite of each other. I was fit and liked to work out. She considered a workout writing two thousand words and reaching for the Oreos.

I could easily run five miles on the treadmill without breaking a sweat. The only place Shelby ran was to the sofa so she didn't miss the next episode of her latest TV obsession.

And she could talk about her 'extra fifteen pounds' all she liked, but I was obsessed with her the way she was. I didn't see the hang-ups she apparently had with her body.

I saw her singing into a fucking mop like she was some nineties heartthrob. I saw her ordering a salad with a pizza because she considered that a balanced meal. I saw her neglecting the things that made her feel good because she had to write right-the-fuck-now. I saw her scribbling into notebooks and sending voice messages and emails to herself because she needed to get the idea down right now.

Shelby was more than she valued herself at, and I'd die trying to show her that.

Shit.

Maybe Sean was right.

Maybe I was in love with her.

Or if I wasn't there, I was well on my way. I already knew I was falling. Like a fucking avalanche.

It was easier to not put it into words. To say I had feelings for her was so much more manageable than putting a real label on how I felt, especially since I knew she wanted to take it slower.

She wanted a natural progression of the relationship. That was never going to happen, but that didn't mean I had to stand under a moonlit sky and profess my undying love.

Shit. She'd probably kick me in the balls.

And the very thought of that made me laugh like hell.

"What's so funny?" Sean asked, eyeing me with confusion.

"Me," I replied, looking in the direction of the entrance to the pier right as two familiar figures appeared.

Shelby and Brie were walking close together. Brie's black hair made Shelby's brown hair look brighter than usual, and as they got closer, I could see that they had their arms linked and their heads close as they talked.

Something flipped in my stomach.

Fuck—was I nervous?

I was.

This was only our second date if you went on a technicality, and while this was a setup we'd done before, I'd never considered holding her hand or being, well, a couple with her.

Shit.

Shelby's face lit up as she laid eyes on me.

And just like that, the nerves disappeared.

This was Shelby. My crazy, passionate, sarcastic, kooky girl. Whether she was my roommate or my best friend or something else, she'd always be that.

My girl.

It was a weird realization, but I was oddly comfortable with it. It rolled off the brain, never mind the tongue.

Brie bounded up to Sean and wrapped her arms around him, kissing him passionately.

Shelby approached me much more casually. She was almost shy with her cheeks flushed a light pink and her dark brown eyes shining but focused on the planks beneath our feet instead of on me. "Hey," she said quietly.

I grinned.

Grinned. Like. Fuck.

"Hey," I said back. "Good dinner?"

"It was good until my dad heard me say you were good in bed."

Excuse me?

She jerked her head up and clapped her hand over her mouth, her eyes wide. If it were possible, her entire face was redder than just a minute ago.

I laughed low, taking a step toward her. "Must have

been awkward."

"Mhmm." She finally met my eyes. "He couldn't look at me until I left."

"Can't wait to see him next," I drawled. "I specifically promised I wouldn't take advantage of you."

"Well, to be fair, I dragged you into my room." Shelby shrugged. "Although that might not work in your favor, either."

"I'll take it." I smiled and dipped my head to kiss her. Her lips were soft and tasted like chocolate and coconut, and I knew exactly which dessert she'd picked at the bar. "You had your mom's cheesecake without me."

"She kept you three slices." Her lips twitched. "Apparently, she wasn't nearly as bothered about us having sex as my dad was."

"That's because she's been plotting your wedding since you were sixteen," Brie quipped, ruining the moment. "Her and Georgina, that is."

"What?" I raised my eyebrows.

"Oh, yeah. They've been plotting it for years. It's why nobody is surprised." She let go of Sean's hand and walked over to us. "You're so close that everyone assumed you had this brother-sister thing going on, right? But your moms thought there was something more, and now I think they were onto something." She shrugged. "They had a literal bet on you two getting it on. Kinda weird, but—"

"Get to the point, Brie," Shelby said, a slight edge to her tone.

"All right. They figured you were both so protective over the other that nobody would ever pass The Test, as they called it—capital letters and all—so they bet that

245

you'd both get together by the time you were either twenty-five or thirty." She paused and looked at me. "I think your grams won that one. Shelbs, your mom called thirty, but Georgina thought it'd be twenty-five. Since you're twenty-six, Jay, Grams just won like eight-hundred bucks."

"How do you know that?" Sean asked.

Brie met his eyes. "Your mom. They're all in it together."

"And you never told me?"

"Well, no. I was sworn to secrecy when I heard them talking about it."

"You never told me?" Shelby squeaked. "Best friend my ass!"

"I picked forty!" Brie held her hands out, palms up. "I thought you'd both be forty and divorced before you figured it all out."

If Shelby's gaze was deadly, Brie would be six feet under.

"It's so nice to know we have parents who care about our feelings. Friends, too," I said dryly. "I wish I was surprised."

"Same," Shelby muttered. "No wonder your mom always brought out the baby pictures."

"Like you hated that."

"Hush." She spun and pushed a finger against my lips. "I think we can accuse your mom of influencing the vote. Grams, too. She's always been one for getting out the submarine picture."

Sean sniggered at the same time Brie looked away.

"On another note," I said brightly. "If anyone had to

be right, at least it was Grams. We can guilt her into food forever."

Shelby perked up at that. "Oh, she so has to hand over that spaghetti recipe now."

"You mad?"

Shelby's hair whipped around her face until she swept it around the back of her neck. "I want to be. I think I should be. Don't you?"

I nodded. "I feel like our parents are shits for betting on something we had no plan of happening. It was never in our plans to feel this way, but we do."

"We do." Her throat bobbed as she agreed. "Do you feel like we're pressured into making this work now? Because I do. I feel like we have to because of them."

I twisted my head until I looked at her. We were both standing halfway down the pier, somewhere between the hook-a-duck stall and the fortune teller, and the wind was just bearable.

And I could see it. On her face. The worry. The pressure. The expectation.

I moved closer to her so our elbows touched. "No."

"No?" She tilted her head.

Our eyes met.

"No," I repeated. "I don't care what they think. I think their betting pool is stupid and petty, and I am not surprised Brie threw her own bet in. She thought it'd take us until forty, remember?"

She nodded. "It's hard enough, isn't it? It's not like we can just throw our friendship away. I'm worried that's what will happen if we dive headfirst into this."

"I'm worried we'll lose it if we don't."

"Really?" She grabbed the edge of the pier, her knuckles going white.

"Yeah." I turned sideways and rested my elbow on the cold surface. "Shelbs, I don't care what they think. You're my best friend. I think we can make a relationship work because of that."

She met my eyes. "Doesn't it make you feel weird that everyone has been betting for us?"

"A little, and I'm going to tell them exactly what I think of that." I half-smiled. "But they can bet all they like. It doesn't matter to me. What matters to me is you. You've always been the person who matters the most. The way I feel about you now compared to two years ago is just semantics."

"So you're saying this is just an evolution of our feelings; an amplification of what was already there?"

"No. Two years I didn't want to grab your face and kiss you every time I saw you. That's a new development." My half-smile became a whole one. "Maybe there was an underlying feeling for both of us. I don't know. I'm not a psychologist. But I do know something."

"What's that?"

"There's nobody I'd rather fuck up with than you."

She laughed, dropping her head. Waves crashed against the pier, but when she didn't move, I joined her, making it so she had to loop her arm through mine.

"You make me all kinds of happy, Shelbs. We don't need to define what we are to each other right now."

She took my hand, brushing her thumb over the back of my hand. "I'm thinking too much again, aren't I? I know in my mind that this can work. It sounds so crazy when a week ago, telling you how I felt was the stupidest thing I could do. I'm starting to think that your mom getting me drunk had a purpose."

"In her defense, it worked."

"It really did." She leaned into me, laughing. "I'm scared, Jay. I'm scared that the things you laugh at me about now will be annoying in a year. I'm afraid to lose your friendship, because that's the most important thing ever. I wasn't lying when I said I trust you—I do. I really do, more than anyone, and that goes for anything."

"You won't ever lose me."

"You don't know that."

"I do." I straightened, pulling her up with me.

She met my eyes. Bright lights from the rides and lights on the pier danced across her face, and I cupped her jaw with my hands. My thumbs brushed her cheeks as the lights did, illuminating everything from her downturned lips to her high cheekbones to the rich brown of her beautiful eyes.

"Listen to me." I closed even more distance between us. "No matter how badly I tease you or we fight, you will never lose me. Your friendship is everything to me, no matter how I feel about you. I'll take a broken heart over losing you. Just know this; no matter how we feel, no matter what happens, what we have is too strong to break. I'll hound your ass until I die and then some."

She turned her cheek into my hand, laughing softly. "I have fun with you, you know that? I never thought it would happen, but dating you has been so fun."

"Brie and Sean left already. You wanna ride the teacups and get some cotton candy?"

She immediately brightened. "Are you kidding? Brie hates the teacups. They're my jam."

"Brie hates them because they move at the speed of her brain." I linked my fingers through Shelby's, pulling her after me. "And before you say it, cotton candy is the only thing I will accept that's pure sugar."

"Bitch, please." Shelby snorted. "You put pure sugar in your coffee every morning!"

"Did you just call me a bitch?"

"In the nicest way possible."

"There is no such thing."

"Welcome to dating me. I use all my brain power when I write. Anything between the hours of eight p.m. and eleven a.m. is not subject to filtering."

I glanced back at her. "Does that mean you can talk dirty then?"

"Why? Are you lacking in that department?" Her eyes sparkled, her lips curving. "Because I can recommend some books if you are."

I tugged her into my side and wrapped an arm around her waist, anchoring her against me. "Not at all. I was just wondering if you partook in the activity."

"Partook in the activity?" She leaned into me and giggled as we walked. "Excuse you, William Shakespeare. Have you been reading?"

"Only the sports news." I directed around a group of teens who weren't paying attention to their surroundings. "I was trying to be dignified."

"Picking up socks is dignified."

"I picked up the fucking socks!"

Shelby laughed, wrapping both arms around my waist and stopping us dead in the middle of the pier. She beamed up at me, her hair in loose waves, her brown eyes stripped back to show how much she loved this.

"I know." Her smile only widened as she tightened her grip on me. "You know, I don't care."

"About what?"

"About anything," she replied. "About the bets our family apparently set."

"Really?"

She nodded. "They threw me for a minute, but I really don't care, not when I think about it. We had the best date ever."

"You did wear heels for me."

She extracted herself from my arms for a second to mock-curtsey. "And you appreciate what I did. That's teamwork, you know?"

I pulled her back to me and kissed her forehead. "Is it teamwork if you wash my shorts from now on?"

"Is it a communal laundry basket? That's a real issue."

"Does it need to be?"

"If you think I'm doing yours and mine…"

"No!" I laughed, holding her tighter when she tried to level me with a dark look. "One wash a week. Each. Is that fair?"

She leaned back just enough to eye me. "We need a new chore chart. And a new meal plan. And—"

"Shut up."

I kissed her. She squealed, but I didn't care. She had an awful lot of time to talk about her to-do lists and her chore plans and her meal plans and whatever else she needed to make her life be organized. I laughed because she was such a flighty person with her imagination, yet she needed control over every other aspect.

That could be figured out.

Today.

Tomorrow.

Next week.

It would be done.

For now, we could abide by the rules we had. That no pants were the best pants. That Oreos had to be labeled. That bathroom doors had to be locked. That the feather duster was my friend. That we both had to clean our hair out of various sinks and drains.

I'd figure out the vacuum tomorrow.

I'd put a pen next to the notebook on the windowsill in the bathroom.

I'd work out how exactly to load the dishwasher next week.

I'd replace the candle she liked to burn while she wrote next month.

I didn't care. I didn't care about chores or routines or rules as long as she believed in us, and by the way she kissed me back, she did.

She kissed me hard, in the middle of the pier, surrounded by a bunch of people.

It wouldn't be easy. It'd be hard, in fact. So hard. But she was the one who wrote romance. If anything, she was more prepared for this than I was.

All I knew was that I was standing here with my arms around my best friend as she kissed me back. As she sent fire through my veins and desire straight to my cock.

As she brought her body so hard against mine through tiny giggles that I knew that, somehow, somewhere, at some point, we'd be totally fucking okay.

She wrapped her arms around my neck.

I gripped her ass.

And I smiled against her lips as she did the same.

Yeah.

We were gonna be just fine.

EPILOGUE

The Future Includes A Hot Tub

Shelby

Three Years Later

The door to the apartment swung open.

Jay appeared in all his glory. His hair hadn't changed, and he wore the uniform of a white tank top that showed off his tanned biceps and a pair of gray sweat shorts that did things to a girl's clitoris.

"Jay!" I squealed, making a run for him.

His green eyes widened. He was only just ready as I launched myself at him and clamped onto him like a shellfish. My legs went around his waist as my arms circled his neck. Together, we staggered back into the hallway as he cupped my ass to hold me in place.

"That's what I call a welcome home." He laughed, steadying us both. "Hi to you, too."

"I have the best news!" I bounced as he carried me

back into the apartment.

"So will my cock if you don't get on with it."

I blushed and jumped down. "The publisher bought my book!"

His eyebrows shot up. "No way! They finally agreed?"

"Yes!" I threw myself at him again, and this time he was ready for me.

He spun me around. My legs flew through the air as his arms clamped tight around my waist, holding me flush against him.

"Why didn't you call me?" he demanded, setting me down.

"I got the final email like twenty minutes ago!" I bounced on the balls of my feet. I was a ball of nervous and excited energy. This was a dream I didn't know I had, but the publisher had agreed to put my books on shelves, and while I knew this wasn't a guarantee, it was a nice thought.

I didn't know what would happen. It was that simple. But in the last five years, I'd learned that not knowing was the best policy.

I'd evolved from ghostwriting. Two years of working hard had finally established my name as an author, and I'd been able to give up writing for other people. Jay had been nothing but supportive the day I'd sat him down and told him I wanted to write for me. He'd picked up the slack in the apartment when I'd been on a deadline or I just couldn't stop writing.

He'd loaded dishwashers and emptied vacuums and bleached toilets and polished tables.

All alongside his own job.

His dad was preparing to retire and hand the reins over to Jay. It meant he wouldn't just manage one gym, but six. Across the state. Cutting down our time together.

The good thing about what I did was that I could do it anywhere. And the advance I'd been given—while meager—was enough to top up the money we'd saved in the past three years.

"Listen—actually, no, look!" I grabbed my phone from the coffee table and unlocked it before I shoved it in his face.

His eyes scanned the screen. "Are you serious?"

I nodded. "I already calculated taxes based on what my agent said and our projected incomes."

"You little nerd."

"Shut your mouth. We can buy a house!"

He plucked the phone from my hands. Grinning, he slid his fingers into my hair and planted his lips on mine. "You sure?"

I nodded, never taking my mouth from his. "One hundred percent. We're over-budget, actually. We saved a lot living together."

"Mhmm. I was going for that all along."

"Sure you were." I wrapped my arms around his waist, laughing. "You were a poor little twenty-something ass who couldn't do his own laundry and inadvertently starting a family betting pool about when we'd finally get together."

"And if you'll remember," he said, circling his arms around my waist. "We were the eventual winners because everyone was wrong."

I pressed my face against his chest. He was right. We'd found out the parameters of the bets were tighter than we'd been led to believe, so we'd demanded the eight hundred dollars in winnings and put that cash into a piggy bank until we'd figured out what to do with it.

It'd taken us a year, but we'd finally found the house we wanted. It was a few miles down the road on the coast and needed some serious TLC, but we were ready for whatever was thrown our way.

"You're right. They were wrong." I slipped my hands up his muscular body and wrapped my arms around his neck, taking a look at the ring on my left hand. "I mean, they thought we'd both be thirty by the time you finally got on one knee."

Jay laughed, burying his nose in my hair. My freshly-washed hair, if you please. There was something to be said for secretly planning to marry your best friend.

"How much longer are we going to keep them guessing?" he said into my ear.

"Not sure." I turned my face into his. "Who guessed that we'd keep it secret for six months?"

"Nobody." He brushed his lips over mine. "You know they'll take secret bets on the wedding?"

"I know."

"Are we eloping, then?"

"Can you imagine the carnage if we disappeared for a weekend and came back married?"

He paused, tilting his head to the side. "Vegas, then?"

Laughing, I leaned right back. "The Bellagio does have rooms available this weekend."

His green eyes captured mine, dancing with the laughter I'd come to love so much. "You book the hotel, and I'll book the flights."

I grinned and walked back. "I'm still taking photos of you with your little submarine."

"That is how you show me you love me," he replied, his expression mirroring mine. "And to show you how much I love you, I have a video of the pageant you auditioned for when you were eight."

I gasped. "I'm rethinking how much I love you."

"You can try." He smacked his lips together in an air-kiss. "But I'll always be the guy who picked up his socks and bought you unicorn stickers for when you hit your word count."

I turned and walked backward. "You play dirty, Cooper."

He grinned. "You want a sticker for that observation, the future Mrs. Cooper?"

"Watch your mouth," I warned him. "I might love you, but I'm not above giving you a Post-It warning everyone that your ass belongs to me."

"That's one sticker I'll wear with pride." He smirked. "As long as there isn't a smiley-face on it."

My lips tugged up. "Nope. It'll be a sad face."

His laughter followed me into our room, and I managed to keep mine under wraps until I was alone.

Dear Past Shelby:

Falling for your best friend?

It's not such a bad idea after all.

THE ACCIDENTAL GIRLFRIEND

COMING JULY 25th!

Top Tip: Don't put out an online ad offering your services as a fake date. Someone *will* take you up on it.

And it won't just be for one night.

And that, ladies and gentleman, is how I ended up being Mason Jackson's fake girlfriend.

He didn't even want me to be. No—his sister was solely responsible for me being his date for his ten-year high school reunion.

Now, she's responsible for telling his parents our relationship is real.

We have no choice. We have to act like this isn't all a mistake, like it's not all fake, like we're totally, completely, utterly, head-over-heels in love with each other.

Simple, right?

Wrong.

ABOUT THE AUTHOR

Emma Hart is the *New York Times* and *USA TODAY* bestselling author of over thirty novels and has been translated into several different languages.

She is a mother, wife, lover of wine, Pink Goddess, and valiant rescuer of wild baby hedgehogs.

Emma prides herself on her realistic, snarky smut, with comebacks that would make a PMS-ing teenage girl proud.

Yes, really. She's that sarcastic.

You can find her online at:

www.emmahart.org

www.facebook.com/emmahartbooks

www.instagram.com/EmmaHartAuthor

www.pinterest.com/authoremmahart

Alternatively, you can join her reader group at http://bit.ly/EmmaHartsHartbreakers.

You can also get all things Emma to your email inbox by signing up for Emma Alerts*.

http://bit.ly/EmmaAlerts

*Emails sent for sales, new releases, pre-order availability, and cover reveals. Each cover reveal contains an exclusive excerpt.

BOOKS BY EMMA HART

Standalones:
Blind Date
Being Brooke
Catching Carly
Casanova
Mixed Up
Miss Fix-It
Miss Mechanic
The Upside to Being Single
The Hook-Up Experiment
The Dating Experiment
Four Day Fling
Best Served Cold
Tequila, Tequila
Catastrophe Queen
The Roommate Agreement

The Vegas Nights series:
Sin
Lust

Stripped series:
Stripped Bare
Stripped Down

The Burke Brothers:
Dirty Secret
Dirty Past
Dirty Lies
Dirty Tricks

Dirty Little Rendezvous

The Holly Woods Files Mysteries:
Twisted Bond
Tangled Bond
Tethered Bond
Tied Bond
Twirled Bond
Burning Bond
Twined Bond
The Holly Woods Files Mysteries Boxset, 1-4
Tricky Bond (A Short Story)

By His Game series:
Blindsided
Sidelined
Intercepted

Call series:
Late Call
Final Call
His Call

Wild series:
Wild Attraction
Wild Temptation
Wild Addiction
Wild: The Complete Series

The Game series:
The Love Game
Playing for Keeps
The Right Moves
Worth the Risk

Memories series:
Never Forget
Always Remember

WITHDRAWN

CPSIA information can be obtained
at www.ICGtesting.com
Printed in the USA
LVHW011133120519
617538LV00001B/172/P

9 781091 463387